Wind Cave

John Eric Ellison

Fifth Edition

978-1-63821-473-1

Thanks to:

Lisa Lindburg of the Deschutes County Sheriff's Department. April Huey, working for the Redmond, Oregon, Sheriff's Department. Greg Brown, for information given while he was Sheriff. Special thanks to Bob Young, Milt Newhouse, and Fred Northway. Martha Pyle and Kevin Barclay of the Deschutes County Library were enthusiastic and invaluable. Irv Wiswall— thanks for your interest and the photos used for illustrations. Roger Brandt shared his helpful caving experiences. Paul Steward for help with the layout. Also, thanks to several employees from the Oregon Bureau of Land Management and Forestry Service.

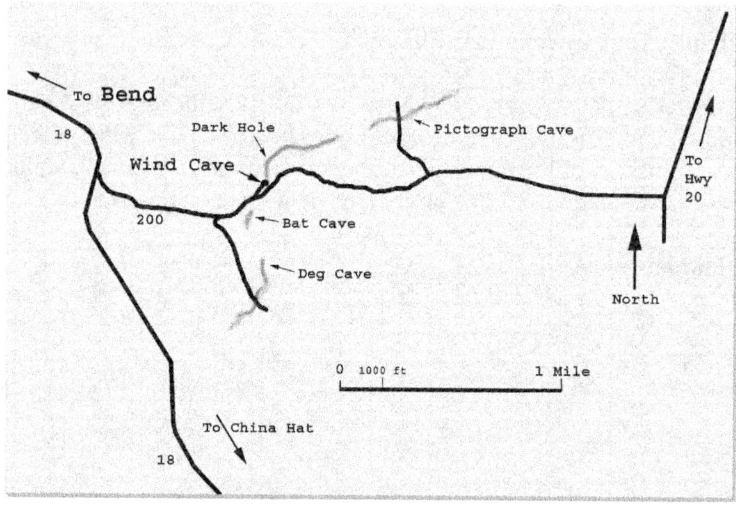

Contents:

Wind Cave

Wind Cave, Dark Hole
Poorly fenced after
the events of 1969

Bend, Oregon
March 1969

Beverly Winston lifted and removed the quilted chair coverlet and nestled herself into her recliner. She didn't mind Missy lounging around wherever she chose. Preferring not to brush the chair for Persian cat hair she kept it covered. The cat enjoyed her owner's favorite chair as much as Beverly did. Missy also loved her designated spot on a quilted pillow in front of the fireplace. Beverly made this especially for her and chose pastel hues for the cushion that closely resembled the colors of the coveted throne.

She folded the quilt and placed it on the magazine rack beside her chair, then draped her soft flower robe over her shoulders and smoothed her pink gown. Missy purred softly in front of the fire.

It was well past sundown, and her windows were dark behind closed drapes. An ornate screen covered a warm crackling fire in the fireplace. Before she'd entered the living room, she placed a pot of water on the stove for tea. Soon she would hear it rumble on the stove as the water came to a boil. The sound would be loud enough to hear even when she was deeply engrossed in her reading. Beverly sighed. To the right of the fireplace, the television was somewhat out of place in this Norman Rockwell setting. She seldom turned it on although her son, Thomas, enjoyed it.

She switched on the table lamp next to her left arm. Her hand then settled on the latest National Geographic magazine still in its brown wrapper. She pulled it out of the sleeve and enjoyed the cover. The March issue featured three sea scallops escaping from a starfish. Her mind longingly drifted back to the days when her husband was alive. They used to frequent the beaches at Carmel by the Sea, and Point Lobos, just south of Carmel. She opened the magazine to the cover article and started to read aloud to Missy, but when she looked up to see if Missy was enjoying it, she was nowhere to be seen. Where had she gotten to so quickly? She was on her pillow only moments before. Beverly lowered the magazine and looked around for her cat. That was strange. Now what had managed to distract Missy's attention away from the cozy fire?

A scraping noise outside her living room window captured her attention. "Missy?" she whispered. There was no response. Her son, Thomas, was visiting from California for a while, but he was supposed to be out of town with friends for a couple of days. It wasn't him out there was it? She couldn't see outside, because her windows were closed with blinds drawn. She thought, *Was that the habit of an old woman, or just prudence? Fifty-five. Was that old?* Sometimes the realization of her age numbed her with melancholy. There was a time in her twenties when she considered thirty-five to be old.

Flickering light from the fire began to disturb her with long dancing shadows. Typically, this would not have bothered her. She called out to Missy, then stood up and glanced around the room. The leg brace she wore on her right leg, due to a degenerative disease, squeaked slightly. Beverly mentally cursed the little noise, which seemed all the louder in the oppressive silence that closed in on her when she stopped moving. This was a small house with only two bedrooms, one bathroom, a living room, and a kitchen/dining area. There wasn't much room for a cat to play and hide. She could see her open bedroom door from the living room. The lights were off in that room, which she expected. Like closing windows and blinds, she'd developed the habit of turning lights out when she left a room. There was a cool breeze coming from somewhere. Odd. The front and back doors were closed, and as far as she knew, all of the windows were shut tight as well. What could be causing the draft?

She studied the open bedroom door a moment longer and then called out to Missy again before sauntering over to her bedroom. The smell of potpourri she placed in bowls all over the house masked another scent. One she would later wish she hadn't overlooked. It was subtle gasoline and oil smell. When she entered the bedroom, the first thing she noticed was the window drapes fluttering by the side of the bed. What in the world had Missy jumped outside through this window? More importantly, why was the window open in the first place? She remembered closing it earlier today and was sure of that.

Near the window was her dresser. On top of the furniture were several photos of her when she was young, dressed in her pink ballerina's tutu and ballet slippers. She had been a lovely young woman and talented. Now she was middle-aged, widowed, and missing her only companion, cat.

Her mind felt clouded by confusion. She looked down and noted that the small music box she kept on her dresser was on the floor. She was relieved to see that the little ballerina on its lid hadn't broken in the fall. She thought, *Was Missy to blame for this? Of course, she was.* Missy must have jumped up onto the dresser and then climbed out the window. She noted that two of the photos had been knocked over. Why hadn't she heard them fall? She shook her head. Her hearing wasn't the best, as Thomas pointed out often enough. Oh well, Missy couldn't be blamed for wanting some fresh air, but that meant she'd have to open the front door and call her back in.

Beverly still could not figure out why the window was open. Did she absently forget to close and lock it? She thought *this is a sign of age, old girl.* The corners of her mouth tugged in a rueful smile. *And, you're not as light on your feet as you once were.* She pulled the window down and locked it, then went back into the living room and cautiously opened the front door. It was dark, too dark. Were the streetlights out? She'd have to call the city about that in the morning.

Wasn't the first time the neighborhood streetlights had failed. The last time this happened, Franklin, the only other fifty-something resident on the street other than herself, called the city and was told that they were performing repairs in that area. Surely, they weren't going through THAT again. She thought, *Goodness, that was a noisy time around here. But then, I guess that's why we pay taxes.*

She shrugged and called out to Missy very softly at first and then louder as she grew bolder. To her relief, Missy appeared out of the night and quickly scampered up the sidewalk to the front porch. She slid past Beverly as she entered the house. Beverly was relieved as she watched Missy slink over to the fireplace and begin kneading the pillow with her front paws. She closed and locked the door, then walked over and squatted to stroke her soft fur. Her leg brace squeaked as she knelt. The open window came back to haunt her. That was so unlike her to leave the window open.

She was startled by a banging sound in the kitchen. Her head snapped up, and then she laughed at her raw nerves. It was only the teapot, boiling on a loose burner. Standing, she walked into the kitchen as quickly as her stiff legs would allow and removed the pot from the stove before turning it off. The house was deathly quiet again.

Beverly removed a cup and saucer down from the cupboard

and looked back at Missy. Her cat was shivering and darting nervous glances around the room. It wasn't cold enough inside to cause Missy to tremble like that. She recalled that Missy had a nervous condition she'd developed over the years. *We all get old, now don't we, dear?* Chose a tea bag from a drawer and dropped it into the cup, then poured hot water over it. As she poured, she thought about the scraping noise she'd heard outside the house. *That must have been Missy playing around.* She smiled to herself and felt a little foolish for being such a fraidy cat.

She stepped into the living room with a little light conversation directed toward Missy about the day's weather. Setting the cup and saucer on the lamp table, she prepared to sit down when the lightly pungent smell of gasoline finally drew her attention back to her open bedroom door. Beverly moved in that direction and realized the smell was stronger toward the bedroom. Why hadn't she noticed it before? She straightened and frowned. Her son Thomas smelled like that after working on her tan '65 Dodge.

She muttered aloud, "Thomas must have left some of his dirty work clothes around here somewhere. I wish he'd stop doing that." The sound of her voice brought her some fleeting comfort. Her hands absently touched a few of the familiar things around her. The brick above the fireplace felt warm. Usually, that warmth would be welcome, but right now she was sweating with nameless dread, and the fire only made her sweat all the more. Her heart was pounding as she reluctantly admitted to sensing an unwelcome presence in her home.

"Is someone there?"

She could practically hear her blood coursing through her ears, and she felt her skin tighten from apprehension. The back of her neck and arms prickled as she tasted hot bile in her throat.

She bent over to pick up a fireplace poker and held it for a moment while staring at it as though she feared the need to use it for self-defense. Why was she feeling this way? She shook her head at that ridiculous notion and replaced it into its holder.

She strolled to the guest bedroom where Thomas was temporarily staying. It was as dark and empty as she expected it to be. *Well, old girl,* she thought. *That's enough of this spooky stuff. Sit down, drink your tea, and go to bed.*

Then there was a thud in her bedroom.

Her heart skipped a beat, and her breathing stopped.

"If someone is there, come out at once!" she demanded.

Beverly considered the sound for a moment. It wasn't Missy, and she thought she remembered to close the window in her bedroom so that the wind wouldn't account for that thump. Perhaps it was something Missy had disturbed when jumping out of the window and it had only now fallen. She hoped she wouldn't find anything broken. Gathering her wits and courage, Beverly stepped cautiously into her bedroom. This time she flicked on the wall switch that controlled the bedside lamp. No light. She flicked the switch a couple more times out of frustration. Nothing. *It must be unplugged,* she thought; so, she began inspecting the area around her dresser by the light from the living room.

A pair of booted feet shifted in the shadows, hidden behind her open bedroom door. They slid sideways a little, stepped around the door, and into the room. The heavy footsteps were unmistakable in the silence. Beverly spoke without turning.

"Thomas. Is that you? How did you . . ."

She then turned around and froze, lamenting the poor light, and spoke with a catch in her throat. "Who's that . . . Who's there?"

The figure remained hidden by shadow, but the booted steps

sounded like Thomas. The intruder's build was similar to his as well. Her eyes grew more accustomed to the dim light. Still, she could not make out the face. Was that a black ski mask covering his face or her imagination?

The gasoline smell grew stronger as the figure moved from shadow into the firelight. He was wearing a heavy black jacket. Beverly gasped. It was a black ski mask. Worse yet, he was carrying what looked like a giant hammer, held loosely in one of his gloved hands.

The man lunged forward around the foot of the bed to prevent her from escaping. Beverly screamed. He swung at her head with the flat of the hammer and connected so hard that Beverly felt bone give way and burning pain spread over her scalp. Blood spattered the bed and floor; it ran down her face and neck, soaking into her gown. She reeled sideways and tried to scream again, but the man covered her mouth and hissed, "Shhhhhhhhh."

As the attacker held her, he felt his demons trying to leave him. He thought; *The old man had said they would run into her to make her all the more afraid. If I can keep them in her long enough, they will stay there.* He remembered that the old man also quoted out of the bible about the time Jesus had cast demons into pigs. They remained in the pigs long enough to ride them straight to their deaths and then perhaps on to oblivion. Demons could hide in a living body if the conditions were right. At least that was what the old man had said. Now, a wave of relief flooded through him. That was good. They were leaving him to terrify her. The old man was right.

Beverly heard his hissing command to be silent, but her head hurt, and she was dizzy. Was this Thomas? If it was her son, why would he do this to her? Then she remembered all of the arguments they had over money. New suspicions were added to her frantic terror. She swung her fists as hard as she could in her weakening state and hit ineffectually against the sides of her attacker. She wanted desperately to reach up and tear the mask off his head, but he strengthened his grip around her when she tried. The more she struggled and hit him, the more he groaned with sounds of satisfaction. He didn't laugh or speak. He moaned with pleasure. As far as she could tell, these noises didn't sound like Thomas. During her struggle, she noticed that a strong odor of urine overpowered the smell of gasoline on his clothes. She was sickened as she wondered if it was his, or hers? If she could only hear his voice.

Her head was reeling, but she managed to bite his hand through his glove; which startled him long enough for her to wrench loose of his grip and dizzily dash past him for the bedroom door. The attacker grabbed her by the hair and yanked her backward. The floor was slick from the blood. She fell hard. By now, there was blood all over the floor and on parts of the wall where they'd bumped into it during their struggle. He clubbed her repeatedly on her back and shoulders. His frenzied attacks showered the room with streaks and spattered blood that flew from the head of the hammer. Somehow, she pulled herself up onto her bed. She had no way of knowing that her attacker was enjoying his game of mutilation. He didn't intend to deliver the kill shot until he had to. Beverly's eyes swam and her head throbbed in sharp splintered agony. She fell over the bed and passed out. Her head and body bled profusely all over the sheets and soaked into the mattress.

Her attacker was oblivious to her unconscious state. He continued beating her repeatedly on her shoulders, back, and legs. He rolled her off the bed and onto the hardwood floor. She landed with a thud. A pool of blood quickly formed around her body. He felt her neck for a pulse. She was barely alive. Good.

He hadn't wanted to kill her right off. He admired her stamina and will to live. She had fought him, but she had very little strength left after his first stun blow to her head. He dropped the hammer to the floor, pulled an electric cord out of the wall, and wrapped it around her neck. He cinched it tight and pulled back on it.

Beverly awoke with a start, choking, with her face turning blue and then purple. Her eyes were bulging. Adrenaline pumped through her giving her one last burst of strength. She used her hands to try to pull the wire away from her windpipe. Irritated, the man uttered the only words he'd spoken during the attack. He said, "That's enough," letting go of the wire with one hand and grabbing the hammer that lay nearby with the other. He swung it at her head and connected hard enough to leave a hole, which quickly clogged with blood and brain tissue. Beverly sagged and died instantly.

"Messy," he chuckled, then rolled her onto her back and averted his eyes away from her accusing, lifeless stare. One of the things he'd noticed about her a year ago was that Beverly's eyes reminded him of his Aunt Grace. They were loud, independent, and defiant eyes. Now, they were disappointingly dull and weak, like his mother's had always been. He pushed her eyelids closed with his blood-soaked fingers, then rolled her head away from him in case they reopened in rigor mortis.

He took a deep breath and held it for a moment. What was that acidic taint in the air? He exhaled and noticed Missy cowering behind a chair in the living room. He called to her, but she made a growl of distress and slunk into the kitchen.

The man shrugged and then removed his mask. He tucked it into a coat pocket and then went back to work on Beverly. As he straightened her body, a small music box on the floor caught his eye. A ballerina doll was poised in a pirouette on its lid. He grinned, then stuffed the music box into one of his deep coat pockets; a souvenir. He could relive this again and again; his victory over the demons that had been raging inside him.

Stepping over her body, he reached for the bedside lamp and screwed the light bulb back into its socket. He was glad he remembered to unscrew it. Next, he tore Beverly's bloodied electric blanket off her bed, still warm, and wrapped her in it. The cord he used to strangle her was from this blanket. He left the wire wrapped around her neck to keep it out of the way.

He reached behind the bedroom door and grabbed the gas station coveralls he had hidden to cover his body after he finished his wet work, put them on, and then walked out into the living room, opened the front door, and looked outside. It was late, but no one was walking around since the streetlights were off. He could take credit for that himself. He knew how to disrupt power to the streetlights. Turning out lights was his specialty, as Beverly had just found out.

Her car keys were easy to find. They were above the kitchen sink on the windowsill. He dragged Beverly into the already open garage and put her crumpled body into the trunk of her car. He liked this sleepy little neighborhood. The old man told him everything there was to know about it in preparation for this night. That old biker had been right about the timing as well. There wasn't a soul around to ask questions.

Once in the car, he pulled out into the street and left the garage door open; this was the only part of his plan that he had not fully resolved before now. He and the old man disagreed about where to take her body. The old man told him to take her as far out into the desert as possible. He had also said that he kept most of his enemies in "deep desert, where only the coyotes howl and the wind blows free."

After killing Beverly, he felt a little dazed and intoxicated. It wasn't as though he hadn't slain people before now. That little bitch that had slapped him in Newport a couple of years back, she had it coming. He was clear-headed when he had watched her weaken and the defiance drain out of her eyes. Weakness. He hated weakness.

OK, he thought. *Do I go out to the caves as I'd planned?* He shook his head in an attempt to clear it and drove the speed limit out of town. He had a fright or two when passing a couple of police cars. One of the cops had even waved to him. He laughed and thought; *I should go back and offer to buy him some coffee or something. Then, over coffee, I'll ask him to help me dispose of the body. All this folksy town shit makes me want to puke.*

That brought a wicked smile to his lips.

Once out of town he headed for the Wind Cave, about eighteen miles southeast of Bend. The darkened sky was cloudy, so he could only see what was illuminated by his headlights. A scattering of sagebrush, tumbleweed, small pine trees, and juniper lined both sides of the highway. He rolled his window down, enjoying the desert air. The sweet smell of juniper was almost comforting. Cloudy or not, it was a beautiful night. Perhaps now he would have some time to feel good about his accomplishment; his triumph over weakness. Weakness was the disease at the root of all social ills. Was he becoming a serial killer? He chuckled. Perhaps so. You take one step, and the rest comes easily. He must not overthink beyond the immediate. *Get rid of the old woman and clear your head,* he thought.

He could just as quickly have taken her out and buried her where the old man said to take her, but that was not what he wanted. He chose to let her body be found, eventually. Why? Because he felt something for her, that's why. It was due to a feeling deep inside himself that he could not well define. When he tried, he described it in this way: If Beverly had taken some of his demons away, then he was technically related to her in some fashion. Right? So, he did not want her murder to remain unheralded, although he didn't expect her to be discovered for quite some time. Few people ever look where he intended to bury her. He wouldn't tell the old man though. Not until he had to.

He arrived at the Wind Cave and drove off-road for twenty to thirty yards until he was close enough to the spot he had in mind. This northeastern entrance to the Wind Cave was not easy to spot by daylight let alone after dark. The cave had a main entrance with a small parking lot. A little way into the cave you could see a hole through to the outside, in the roof of the cave. This opening was referred to as "The Dark Hole." If you were to hike and crawl about twenty minutes into the cave, you would end up here, at this small breach in the hillside. Few people ever bothered to go that far back, fewer yet knew about this northeast entrance. It was small and easy to overlook. He counted on this to buy him a little more time before the body was found. Besides, flies and the rotting smell would eventually give her body away.

That last thought made him aware of his unpleasant odor. He clicked on the ceiling light in the car and looked down at himself. When did he piss himself? He remembered doing that while strangling Lorna on the beach outside of Newport. He had also done that to himself when he was a six-year-old kid. This painful memory caused him to wince.

As he recalled it, his Aunt Grace had tied him into a chair and smeared puppy shit on his chest because he had let Ruffy loose in the backyard. Ruffy had just wanted to play. How could he have known that Ruffy would tear up her flower garden? He remembered her voice as she worked the dog crap into his skin. "Rub out the filthy little monsters inside of you. Rub out the demons. Rub them right out of you." He had tried to squirm away from her vengeful poultice, but he was taped securely into a heavy wooden chair so he couldn't move. His small six-year-old body couldn't possibly escape the black electrical tape that secured him, nor spit out the little red rubber ball she had stuck into his mouth. She'd used black tape over his mouth to hold the ball in place.

Grace said, "I told you not to let your dog into my garden, didn't I?"

He could only nod his head and make frantic throat noises. He knew that Grace was as sickened by the smell as he was, but she had gardener's gloves on.

Grace was a tall, skinny, pale, mean witch of a woman. She cared more for the "point I'm making here" than she did the smell. She continued to lecture him as she smeared more of his own dog's mess into his chest. It was sloppy wet and soaking into his pants. He could feel it dripping down his legs. He felt his bladder loosen and give way and smelled the sharp odor of his urine as it mixed with the other bad smell.

She finished emptying the bucket of filth all over him, then stood back to survey her work.

She smiled and said, "You were tough to catch though. I've got to hand you that much. I'll leave a note for your pitiful mother, to tell her to find you here in the basement, in the dark. I'll tell her what you did and why I needed to do this."

He knew he had been wrong to let his dog loose in the back yard, but he couldn't stand hearing him whine about being let off the chain. At least Grace wasn't mean to Ruffy. Grace loved animals. When she had caught Ruffy in the act of tearing up a young plant, she'd tenderly scolded him and put him back onto his chain. As Beverly's killer looked back on this event years later, the chain was comfortable. There was more than enough room for Ruffy to run, especially when it was attached to the clothesline. Both Aunt Grace and his mother had promised to take Ruffy on weekly trips to the beach to let him run and swim. There hadn't been a good reason to let Ruffy off the chain at all.

Out loud, he shouted, "Devil take old Grace!"

He laughed and thought; *Now that I recall it, Grace was well in her rights to scold the demons out of me.*

That brought his mother to mind. He seldom thought of her. She was weak. Over time he had come to hate her for it. His mother was afraid of Grace, her younger sister, and she had good reason to fear her. At the age of 12, Grace had pushed both of their parents over the edge of a cliff, while their parents were holding hands and listening to the surf crash against the massive boulders 100 feet below. Grace had watched in fascination as their bodies exploded on sharp foamy shards of rock. His mother, Patience, had seen her sister sneak up behind their parents. She thought she was playing. Grace's sudden rush to murder came as a cold shock to Patience. After the screams of her parents abruptly died, Patience heard Grace say,

"You always loved her best!" Patience never trusted her after that, but wouldn't confront her either. Grace pretty much ran roughshod over Patience any chance she got. That included the way Grace treated him as well.

The police wouldn't even consider the idea that these two young women could have had anything to do with their parents' death. They were such sweet, innocent, and well-respected young women. It was written off as an accident. After the funeral, both girls received their family home as part of their parents' will. They will also include enough money and investments to keep them from ever having to work if they reinvested wisely.

The killer shook off his anguished memories and pulled

Beverly's body out of the trunk. He dragged her up to the small opening in the cave and buried her just outside the cave opening by piling rocks and dirt on top of her. He had the presence of mind to bring a small shovel, which he'd have to dispose of later. He tenderly patted her rocky tomb with his hand and then nodded with satisfaction, believing that nobody would ever catch him.

He drove Beverly's car back over the red cinder road and returned to her home. He parked the car in her garage and wasted no time in leaving. As he exited the garage, he noted the reddish color on the tires due to the red cinder road. He had no reason to believe anyone would raise questions about it. The red color also reminded him that there might be bloodstains in the trunk. He chuckled and shook his head to clear it. He thought; *Why should I care about blood in the trunk? There's also blood all over the old woman's bedroom, but none of it is mine.*

Salem Heights, March 1969

Ronald Hazelwood listened to his classmate's file into his sixth-grade homeroom. His head was face down with his forehead resting on his arms, crossed over his desktop. In this way, he made a small pocket of solitude to hide his face from the teacher. She probably wasn't looking at him just then, but he preferred his make-believe privacy anyway. He breathed deeply and sighed. The fake wood veneer on his desktop smelled like soapy vinyl and pencil lead. He'd just suffered through one of Mrs. Bolmeir's in-between class lectures. This one was special, and only for him. He had been defending his sister in the schoolyard again during another shouting match with Raymond Cooley, nothing worse than that---so far. But, the principal frowned on angry confrontations of any kind.

Mrs. Bolmeir was told to "give Ronald a stiff talking too." He lifted his blue eyes and peeked over his arms into the room. Dust motes floated in shafts of sunlight. One of a few notorious school bullies, Greg Heinemann—or as Ronald called him "Greg the Sack"—slumped into the room followed by Little Lisa. She was followed in turn by Jimmy the Spit Goblin, Sweet Lorraine, Todd Buttinsky, Jeremy Nash the Brain, Phillip the Spy-Guy, and many others that had earned one of Ronald's unique nicknames.

The classroom door was like a magic filter. From the moment a kid passed through it, all trace of happy chatter and playground fun transformed into hushed paranoid tones designed to escape the teacher's notice. Within a few moments, their voices became whispers. Nervous silence filled the room.

They all felt Mrs. Bolmeir's penetrating gaze as she watched them settle into their seats. Her soft but seemingly unblinking eyes followed her students as they filed into the room. She noted the hot and dusty, candy-scented child smell that always seemed to accompany young children. Her elbows rested on an oversized desk blotter, and she leaned her chin over crossed hands.

She always wore a deceptively severe expression on her face as she watched her class get comfortable. She had the best-behaved homeroom in Salem Heights Grade School. The reason for this was simple. She commanded respect. Mrs. Bolmeir was well-liked, fair, and had a kindly but stern little old lady's face. Her choice of dull and old-fashioned dresses with black shoes lent her an austere appearance. The rubber soles of her footwear had the added benefit of making her one of the stealthiest teachers alive. She could sneak up on you in a second and often did just that.

The sound of school desks opening and closing, squeaking seats, and an occasional whisper tapered off as Mrs. Bolmeir stood and walked around to stand in front of her desk. Greg the Sack—short for a sack of horse manure—sat on Ronald's right. He leaned over to Ron, ruffled Ron's short brown hair, and whispered, "Hey, Ronny, did she clobber you a good one?"

Greg looked hopeful.

Ronny ignored him and sat back in his seat. His long rounded arms dropped into his lap. He regarded Greg a moment with minimal expression. Greg ignored Mrs. Bolmeir and threw a pencil at Ronny.

"OK, geek," Greg complained, "ignore me then, I don't care. You can go to hell."

Ronny did what he always did when The Sack gave him those instructions. Without looking at Greg, he reached down between their two desks and opened an imaginary trap door.

"You go first, Sack . . . scout around awhile."

Greg hated that nickname. He raised his voice.

"I told you not to call me that, creep!"

Snickers and nervous laughter rose on all sides, but neither of the boys spotted Mrs. Bolmeir until it was too late. How she walked down the aisle without either of them noticing was not so much a mystery as a rubber-soled talent. Her ruler smacked them both. Hard. Both boys were left rubbing their reddened forearms as she strolled back to the front of the room. Nothing needed to be said. Greg glared at Ronny, and Ronny smiled back at him.

Homeroom consisted mostly of spelling, English, and reading. It never passed quickly enough. When a bell sounded the end of the period, they were on to lunch—an hour of free time.

Mrs. Bolmeir stopped Ronny on his way past her desk.

"Mr. Barham spoke to Raymond in his homeroom today. Hopefully, he will leave your sister alone from now on." She smiled. "You know, Ronny, Raymond probably has a crush on Myrna."

There was no comfort in that thought. Raymond was just another school jerk like Greg. Why Raymond hadn't earned one of Ronny's famous nicknames had remained a mystery to Ronny. Perhaps it was because Raymond had no personality or standout preferences. He could pin a nickname on his big ears, but that would be beneath Ronny's style.

"Yeah, I know," Ronny said, returning her smile. "I wish he'd stay away from her. He gets too close to her during recess, and she's always waving off his licorice breath."

Wait a minute, he thought. Perhaps that was nickname

material. Whenever some of the kids would walk up the block to buy candy, Batman, Green Hornet, or Get Smart cards, Raymond would always buy those soapy tasting, licorice-flavored smoker's mints called Sen-Sens. Raymond's father smoked and gave them to Raymond from time to time. Ray developed a taste for them.

Mrs. Bolmeir waved Ronny off to lunch. He waved back, stepped into the hall, turned left, and ran straight into Phil, the Spy-Guy.

"Whoa," Spy laughed. "Watch where you're going, Normal."

Ronny pushed him with a friendly shove.

"If you'd get some real glasses instead of those geeky blue taped-up loser specials you wear, you might see me coming."

They fell into step together and joined their hungry chattering classmates on their way to the cafeteria line.

Spy-Guy sprinted ahead, dodged a couple of giggling girls, skidded around the corner to the right, and disappeared. When Ronny turned that corner, there was the skinny, freckled, redheaded, Spy-Guy waiting for him in a lunch line that was already stretched out into the hall.

Spy called out to him. "Come on, Normal! I saved you a place."

Without warning, Ronny's feet were yanked out from under him. He landed on his elbows. His school books were in his homeroom desk; otherwise, they would have flown out of his hands and scattered everywhere. When he stood up and turned around, he saw The Sack just straightening after grabbing Ronny's feet.

His buddies were laughing and slapping each other on the backs and shoulders. Along with Greg, there were three others. Alfred DeMont the Corpse, Tommy Crotch—still wearing the same torn jeans he had worn since the school year started—and

Greg's girlfriend, Linda Lips. She was kind of cute but in a darkly sinister sort of way. She always wore a sneer. That is, any time you could see her through the long black hair that hung down in front of her face.

The tall, lanky Corpse spoke.

"You gotta learn how to walk, Normal."

Ronny ignored him, got up, and dusted himself off.

"What are you doing here, Corpse? You don't eat, do you? Just blood or something. Right?"

Alfred hated Ronny's nicknames as much as Greg did. He shook his fist and yelled, "You call me that again, and I'll pound you."

Spy interrupted and called Ronny over to join him in line.

"Forget them, man. Just get in line. Here comes the Dog."

Ronny ignored any further threats from Greg and his loser friends and joined Spy in the lunch line. Sure enough, Principal Doug Fremont, the Dog, heard the commotion in the hall. He was on his way through the gym, turned temporary cafeteria. The lunch line moved aside to let him through the door. He stood in the hall and placed his chubby hands in his suit pants pockets before confronting Greg and his buddies.

"You four need to get in line and stop this nonsense, or I'll tell Mr. Barham that he'll have some guests during free period."

Mr. Barham always carried a notepad in his shirt pocket. Whenever a student would cross the behavioral line with him, he would pull out the notebook and accompanying ballpoint pen and then threaten to write their names down on it. He always asked the same thing. "Noon?" Then he'd grin while peering over his small wire-frame glasses at the hapless student, or students.

Sack, Lips, Corpse, and the disheveled Tommy Crotch

frowned and mumbled.

Principal Dog had little patience. "Go on," barked the Dog. "Get in line. If you weren't so interested in Ronny, you wouldn't be the last in line. Now would you?"

That day, lunch consisted of hamburger pizza, cottage cheese, mixed vegetables, orange juice, a sherbet and vanilla dessert cup, and milk. Ronny and Spy joined the rest of their friends at a table close to the double doors leading out onto the schoolyard. There were nine kids at the table. Spy sat his tray down next to Jimmy the Spit Goblin, who sat next to Melvin Wad. Melvin could make a spit wad out of anything and find a way to hit nearly anyone he wanted to without being caught. Regardless, and to add to Melvin's solid reputation, girls *liked* Melvin. They said he was cute and they loved the fact that he was learning to play electric guitar and could sing. Everyone at this lunch table knew him to be an all right guy and talented, but more importantly, one heck of a shot with a spit wad. He and Spit Goblin were inseparable friends. Spit Goblin had a disturbing talent that unnerved everyone, including Melvin, and he was in the act of demonstrating it as Ronny sat down next to Spy. Goblin leaned over to Wad and held a hand under Wad's chin, followed by the sound of moans and pleadings that he would not go through with it.

"Yes, yes, yes," said Goblin. "I must---I must; to prove loyalty to my lifelong friend, Lord Melvin Tupps, his Excellency *The Wad*. I will now take the mouthful of vegetables he currently holds masticated within his mouth."

Everyone at the table acted disgusted, but in truth, this was fascinatingly abnormal behavior. They watched despite laughing protests. Wad pushed a fat greenish yellow gob of chewed-up food out through his lips and into the waiting hand of The Spit Goblin.

Goblin chided Wad. "Oh, come on, my lord. Surely you can do better than that."

Wad shrugged and spat a few more bits of vegetables into Goblin's hand. Jimmy nodded approval and without hesitation, or need to aim, threw the spit wad with full force to hit the back of a neck two tables away. This neck belonged to one of Salem Heights most hated bullies, and there were plenty of them. That thin bully spun around and pointed at Goblin with one finger while wiping his neck with his other hand. He yelled something nobody could understand and jumped up to chase Goblin as he ran laughing out of the lunchroom.

Sweet Lorraine Larson, who was sitting across from Goblin, was laughing along with everyone else. She tossed her curly red hair out of her eyes and said,

"Hey, guys, I'm going outside. Who's coming?"

Goblin ran back into the hall, followed closely by his target, wiggled his fingers goodbye to Lorraine in passing and said,

"Don't forget you're next up to bat when we get out of here, gorgeous."

"I won't forget," she replied.

It was baseball season, and Lorraine loved the game. Her father was a professional baseball player, and she was Daddy's girl. She'd come to school dressed in tomboy fashion, ready for a chance to imitate her old man at the bat.

The only other girl at the table was Little Lisa Brown. She and Lorraine were close friends. Lisa followed her everywhere. After the girls were gone, Spy followed Lorraine with his eyes.

"How come we don't have any girls in K.A.U.S?" Spy pronounced this as a single word, Kaus.

Goblin spoke for everyone at the table.

"Good question, my man. Let's take a vote. Everyone here

in favor of admitting Lorraine and Lisa into the club says, aye."

Jeremy the Brain, Wad, Louis the Eyeball, Pokerface Tim, and Ronny, all remained silent. Spy and Goblin were the only two out of seven that said, "Aye."

Goblin was disgusted. "Why? What's wrong with you guys?" he demanded. "Sweet will fit right in."

Louis the Eyeball rolled his oversized eyes and reached up to knock a stringy lock of blond hair out of his eyes.

"Why?" Eyeball answered. "Because when you vote for Sweet, you vote for Lisa. Sweet and Lisa go practically everywhere together. I mean, Lisa's OK as far as girls go, but I don't think she could handle the stress of our spy club. Besides, with Lisa that would give us an odd number of members again. We've had nothing but bad luck and a lot of trouble from KRSPY since Rock left us." K.R.S.P.Y was pronounced as one word, "Krispy."

They all glanced over at a big kid peering at them from several tables away. His black hair was short around the sides and long on top. A shock of hair hung down into his face, giving him an overall appearance similar to a young Clint Walker, the actor affectionately called "The Big Man" by his peers. The kid was Wallace Green. Ronny had dubbed him The Rock. They missed him, but his parents forbade him from hanging out with what they called "Those weird kids who will only get you into trouble." Rock waved, and they all waved back at him before returning to the subject at hand.

Ronny said, "Look; if we let Sweet in, we get Lisa. That's the way it is. Let's vote again."

Jeremy the Brain believed he had the solution to the whole problem. He was jumping up and down with excitement on his side of the bench and raising his hand as though he were in class. His parents always made him wear a white shirt and black tie to school. Why they insisted on this was anyone's guess. His tie had fallen into his pizza with all his bouncing up and down and now sported a touch of pizza sauce.

"I got it---I got it!" Brain announced. "We let Sweet join and tell Lisa she can hang out as a spy trainee. That way she'll have to learn how to be a real spy, or she's out. If we have to kick her out because she can't cut it—well—that's the breaks. Right?"

Everyone wholeheartedly agreed. They called the girls back over. Lorraine and Lisa had already finished their lunch and were just about ready to go out into the schoolyard. When they heard the proposal, Lorraine was delighted, although Lisa was understandably disappointed with being a trainee. She was told,

"That's just the way it has to be," so she accepted. Lorraine did have one demand. She put her hands on her hips and said,

"I want all of you to stop calling me that stupid name Normal gave me. Let us pick our nicknames."

Wad shook his head emphatically and said, "Uh, uh. Normal makes the names. Club rules."

Ronny nodded and said, "Look, I'll come up with something good for you both. No problem. Especially now, since you're now accepted into Spy's exclusive club. Lorraine, you are now a full-fledged member of KAUS, KRSPY Against Us Spies. Lisa, you're in training. Don't worry; you'll get great names." Lisa wanted to know if there was an initiation to go through. All the voices at the table went silent. The boy's smiles turned to expressions of mock concern. Pokerface Tim broke the quiet with one of his usual deadpan replies. His dark features studied the girls for a moment before he said, "The initiation probably won't kill either of you."

With that, Lorraine brightened, although Lisa looked terrified. Lorraine took Lisa by the hand and said, "Come on, we've got a ballgame to play." She yelled back at the boys,

"You guys hurry up. We've got a ball game to play!"

After Lorraine and Lisa were out the door and running through the basketball court into the sunlit field beyond, Brain turned to Tim and asked, "What initiation?"

Everyone else at the table laughed, and Brain smiled. He knew as well as they did that there was no initiation.

A wet spitting noise drew everyone's attention away from the girls. Melvin Wad spits out a large piece of paper he'd bitten off and chewed up from off the top of his ice cream cup, and then he sought the proper delivery system to launch his soggy projectile. While Wad busied himself with a rubber band he had in his pocket; the other KAUS members scanned the room to guess at his target. Wad saved them the trouble by nodding in the direction of Greg the Sack's table. Sack was flirting with Linda Lips.

True to the Wad's style, he launched an accurate shot that nailed Sack with a whack on his neck. Sack held his hand to the wet spot on his neck then spun around to confront his assailant. Everyone at Wad's table was ignoring Sack and were already engaged in a heated discussion over the all-too-popular topic of math assignments. Sack wasn't buying it for a second. He started to get up and then spotted the Dog, casually walking rounds in his direction. Dog's eyes registered the glint of hate in Sack's gaze, and yet he passed on any confrontation. Sack shook a middle finger at Wad, although no one at the KAUS table appeared to notice while choking back their laughter. Inevitably, that stifled laugh turned into the real thing as all seven KAUS members broke out laughing. Sack and his friends were afraid to retaliate. The Dog was standing by the lunch counter, talking with a kid that was complaining loudly about how the milk tasted.

After a few moments, Ronny changed the subject. "Hey,

does anyone know how the art contest turned out? Who won?"

Eyeball answered, "Tina's toothpick model of this school won first place. That's no surprise since she's her teacher's pet." Everyone groaned and agreed. Eyeball continued. "All but two other projects stunk. The two good ones were Buttinsky's matchstick tower and Roger's resin cube and frog parts thing."

Goblin interrupted. "Oh yeah! Those muddy looking gross things in Roger's clear resin cubes were dead frog parts he'd cut up and put in resin molds during shop class. The Dog found out what was in Roger's cube sculpture and Roger was disqualified. They threw his sculpture away! Can you believe that?" Goblin shook his head in disbelief, and added, "Man, that was too bad. I wish I could have bought it. It was way cool!" Goblin spotted Roger at one of the tables. He shouted and waved to get his attention. When Roger looked over at him,

Goblin yelled, "Hey, Roger! Let's make another one!"

Roger seemed to know what he was saying. He smiled, nodded, and then glanced nervously around to see if the Dog had heard.

Goblin turned his attention back to his friends at his table and then continued. "Buttinsky is going to save his tower and light it off on the fourth of July. Too bad he's KRSPY."

By the time Goblin finished talking everyone had piled their garbage on their trays and were getting up to take them over to be washed. Within less than a minute, they were running out the door in the direction of the baseball diamond.

Two girls, not Lisa or Lorraine, stopped Ronny on the way to the game. Ronny told the others to go on without him and that he'd be right there. He nodded to the two girls and asked, "You two need more bloodsucking juice. You're good distributors, but I'm out of it right now."

The youngest girl was a geeky looking fifth-grader by the

name of Betty. She spoke first. "That's not what we want, Normal. We still have lots to sell, but the customers want to know how it works."

The other girl was a cute blond fifth grader named Alice Faye, after a singer/actress her parents liked. She practically begged to be told how the stuff worked. Ronny gave in to her big blue eyes. He said, "OK, OK." He held out a hand. "Do you have any of the stuff with you?"

Alice wasted no time in producing two small vials that Ronny had taped together as part of his packaging. Each vial was about three inches long with a cork stopper. They were filled halfway with a clear liquid. He pointed to each vial and explained. "As you know, you place a drop of one liquid on your skin and then a drop of the other directly on top of the first drop. The two chemicals are different from each other. When they combine, they turn red. The reason it looks like blood is forming on the skin is that the two liquids are not being stirred. They turn red in little spots. If you were to rub them together, they would immediately turn completely red. Get it? It's just a trick. Now don't tell anyone, or they'll quit buying the stuff, and you'll both lose your commissions. OK?"

Betty asked, "Can't you tell us what the chemicals are?" Ronny looked at her as if she was crazy. "No, I can't, and do you know why?"

Alice looked a little hesitant, but answered, "Because you'd kill us if we knew. Right?"

Ronny laughed. "No, no, nothing like that. I'm not like Hawks, with his super-secret spy club name that no one can understand on pain of death. It's just that you might go into business for yourselves or something. Anyone can buy a chemistry set."

That was good enough for the girls, but Ronny had to ask,

"Do you have any more money for me? You should've sold at least two more sets by now, and I need to see what you have left."

Between the two of them, the girls produced a dollar fifty for Ronny at 25 cents commission per set. That meant they had sold two more sets at a dollar each. They should have two sets left, which they did. All was well. The business was picking up.

Ronny nodded approval, then waved goodbye, and ran toward the baseball diamond. He couldn't help thinking about the new products he had in mind. For instance, some of those edible candy bugs he could make with the machine he got for Christmas, and homemade X-ray glasses. He experimented with making the glasses himself. He ordered a pair of X-ray glasses from the back pages of a Green Lantern comic book. When they arrived, he pulled the glasses apart and discovered that they consisted of little bits of feather sandwiched between two pieces of thick paper. It was then glued together with holes for eyes that let you look through the feather. It gave the illusion of a skeleton underneath the person. Of course, it did the same to anything else. Ronny laughed out loud when he thought of the time he inspected Mr. Barham with the X-ray glasses. Who would ever believe that Mr. Barham had a skeleton?

Barham reminded him of a shark swimming through the classroom, with his wide shark-like smile, ready to strike without warning with his pen and pad of paper. "Noon?" Barham would ask. No, sharks had wiggly bones called cartilage, not a skeleton. Ronny mentioned these bones to cartilage comparisons once or twice to a few of his friends, but they only returned his laugh with a blank stare and said, "You're not normal, Normal."

When he got to the baseball diamond, Lorraine yelled at him. "Hey, Normal. You missed watching me strike out, but I'm up again. With you here, I might get the luck!"

Ronny smiled, waved approval, and then sat next to Goblin. He noticed Eyeball and Brain one row down. They were studying one of Eyeball's weird magazines about UFO's and the supernatural. According to Eyeball, Brain was "at it again." Brain was building some ghost tracking gadget from schematics printed in one of Eyeball's magazines. From the looks of what Ronny could see over Brain's shoulder, they were analyzing a schema together. And, of course, arguing about it. Eyeball insisted that he could do a better job with a stick than Brain could do with "this stupid thing," as he put it. Brain countered the jab by asking Eyeball why he bought "rags like this---" He whacked the magazine with the back of his hand. "---if he didn't believe in them." Eyeball said that he didn't believe all of it; just most of it, and those gadgets alone couldn't track the supernatural. Ronny smiled, shook his head, and turned his attention back to the game.

Melvin Wad and Pokerface Tim were the only KAUS members playing ball. The other five watched the game from behind the chain-link fence. It was a good game, but in their opinion, the wrong team was winning. The team with KRSPY members on it was ahead by two runs. Lorraine swung and hit a beauty out into the left field. She made it to second base before an outfielder caught the ball and tossed it ahead of her. The second baseman, Theodore Hawks, caught it too late to stop her slide into base.

Hawks was KRSPY's founder. He was popular and charismatic. Spy couldn't stand the sight of Hawks and his good looks. He always said, "Those KRSPY guys are pricks and deserve a little competition." When Spy enlisted Ronny, Tim, and the others, they asked him why KRSPY needed "competition." Spy only smiled and said, "Because they're here, and they're pricks. That's good enough." Krispy Against

Us Spies, KAUS, was born. And, their sole ambition was to aggravate KRSPY members any chance they got.

No one but Hawks knew what the initials K.R.S.P.Y. stood for, and he wouldn't even tell his members what they meant. He said it was a super-secret, and that he'd have to kill anyone who knew what the initials stood for. One fated day Spy confronted Hawks about the KRSPY name and received the same threatening response everyone else got for the trouble of asking. After Hawks had delivered his usual brush-off, Spy had leaned forward, adjusted his taped-up glasses, got up close to Hawks and laughed right in his face. Hawks was enraged. He whistled, and the other seven KRSPY members ran to converge on the fleeing Spy. Spy continued to laugh like a maniac and outran them all. They gave up the chase when Spy climbed up the hill behind the baseball diamond and then left the schoolyard through a hole in the fence. The fence separated Salem Heights School from a neighboring church parking lot.

Hawks threw the ball back to the pitcher, another KRSPY member by the name of Todd (Buttinsky) Hatcher. He was stocky and looked an evil kind of mean. Of course, Buttinsky was Ronny's tag for him and, of course, Todd hated it.

Pokerface was up to bat. Buttinsky tucked the ball between his knees and then spit into his hands. Lisa and Lorraine both yelled, "Gross!" Todd took the ball and rolled it between his palms while glaring at Pokerface. Pokerface lowered his bat and then brought it up, ready to swing.

Buttinsky wound up and threw the ball to another KRSPY member playing catcher. He was an oily kid with a perpetual grin named Frank Farter. Another tag name. His real name was Porter.

The pitch was good, but the swing was a miss.

"Strike, one!" Frank announced.

Buttinsky stomped the pitcher's mound and spat into his hands again. Frank tossed him the ball. Buttinsky yelled out,

"What was wrong with that pitch, pisshead?"

"I didn't like the looks of it!" Tim yelled back. "Learn how to pitch, moron!"

The muscles in Buttinsky's jawline tightened, and he ground his teeth as he threw another pitch. Pokerface casually swung and connected. The ball sailed over the backfield and into a classroom window, breaking it, and earned him and Lorraine a walk to home base. That tied the score.

The school bell announced the end of recess. Lunch and free period were only an hour total. It always seemed to fly. The tied score mortified Hawks. He walked up next to Ronny as everyone headed back through the schoolyard. He said, "You know, Ronald, I think your sister has a thing for our man Raymond over there. What do you think?"

Ronny continued to ignore him as they approached the concrete portion of the yard. He did glance over to see Raymond staring at Ronny's sister, Myrna. Hawks pursued the issue. "I think Ray's going sweet on her, but she's playing hard to get. Maybe the rest of us KRSPY guys should hold her while Ray gives her the kind of smooch she wants. What do you think?"

There was a whooshing sound, and then a rubbery bang as a basketball suddenly hit Hawks hard on the side of the head, knocking him sideways. Hawks lost his footing and fell to his knees at Ronny's feet. Rock walked up to Hawks and ruffled his hair then retrieved the ball and spun it on the end of an index finger. Hawks jumped up to his feet, shaking his fists at Rock. He shouted, "I'll get you for this, Wallace!" Then he hurried into the building rubbing the side of his head. Gratefully, none of the school officials were watching.

Ronny laughed and waved goodbye to Hawks. He turned

to the smirking Rock standing next to him and said, "Thanks, Rock. I almost decked him myself."

Rock accepted a high five from Ronny. He said that he overheard what Hawks said about Myrna and didn't like it one bit. As they followed Hawks into the building, Rock insisted, "You don't have to worry about your sister while I'm around."

The rest of the school day passed quickly. As usual, all KAUS members met in the gym after the last classes of the day. They performed the obligatory KAUS double-fisted fist butting and went their ways. Spy and Ronny always rode their bikes home together. Spy usually veered off to his place about three-quarters of the way to Ronny's house. Today, the two of them exited the gym to the schoolyard and headed for the outside corner of the building toward the bike rack. The schoolyard swarmed with kids lining up to catch their busses. Sounds of excitement and minor confrontations filled the dusty air. Rattling bikes being unchained could be heard from around the corner to the left. As they rounded the corner, they ran straight into three KRSPY members. Raymond Cooley, Hawks, and Larry Powers, a new guy transferred from Bend, Oregon. Larry seemed friendly enough. No one knew what Larry was doing with Hawks. Suspicions were that Hawks was trying to get him to join KRSPY.

Raymond moved in front of Ronny, blocking his bike.

"Where's your sister, Normal?"

"Get away from my bike," Ronny replied.

Raymond remained undaunted. "I said, where's your sister, Myrna? All I want is a little kiss; that's all."

As fate would have it, Myrna rounded the corner right behind Spy. She nearly dropped her books when she saw Raymond. The tableau froze for a moment. Myrna shifted her books to one arm and stepped between Ronny and Spy. She raised a small fist and held it under Raymond's chin.

"You stop threatening my brother and me," she demanded defiantly.

Cooley and Hawks laughed at her and mocked her words in a whining voice. Larry smiled at the girl's defiance.

Raymond didn't like being threatened by a girl. He pushed her. Ronny reacted immediately. He dropped his books and lunged at Raymond. He shoved him backward away from Myrna and then stepped behind Ray. Before Raymond could regain his footing, Ronny threw one of his arms around Raymond's chest and grabbed Raymond behind the knees with his other arm. Ronny pulled and lifted Raymond against his chest and into the air in one variation of a fireman's carry. He'd learned this move in the YMCA and had been wondering when he'd get a chance to use it. After that, he carried the kicking and screaming Raymond out beyond the bike racks trying to decide what to do with him. Ray repeatedly tried to hit him. Ronny managed to dodge most of the blows to his head but sustained several to his back and sides. At this point, all the kids in the schoolyard were aware of what was going on. The busses had started to arrive.

Despite the arrival of the busses, all of the kids circled Ronny and Raymond. The usual shouts of, "Fight! Fight!" was everywhere. Myrna was in tears. Ronny was in tears himself due to the blows Raymond managed to land successfully. Hawks stepped forward to intervene and help Raymond. To Hawks, this embarrassing situation looked terrible for any KRSPY member and certainly set the wrong example. Nobody should get away with humiliating a KRSPY member.

Hawks shouldered through the crowd. Just before he could lend his support to Raymond, he felt a heavy restraining hand fall onto his shoulder. He spun around and came face to face with Rock. Hawks tried to shake the hand away, but Rock countered by grabbing him by both shoulders and pulling him over Spy-Guy's outstretched foot that just coincidentally appeared in front of Hawk's feet. Hawks fell over Spy's foot. That was enough for Hawks. He jumped to his feet and shouted a threat above the noise before running off in disgrace.

"I told you I'd get you, Rock, and I mean it!"

Rock waved him off without so much as a word, then turned back to watch the fight. He pushed through the crowd and witnessed what he later called one of the coolest things he'd ever seen. Ronny finally gave in to Raymond's demands to be let down. He lifted Raymond just slightly, and then shouted, "Fine!" and rudely tossed Ray to the ground. Raymond landed with a grunt at the feet of Chuck Tenant.

Raymond looked up and saw Chuck's usual black denim pants and jacket. He was too embarrassed to look into Chuck's face. Chuck was considered the coolest guy in school. Not even Ronny dared to give Chuck a nickname. The name "Chuck" was enough to inspire respect around the school. Chuck loomed over Ray as Raymond struggled to his feet and spun around to see where Ronny was. He was nowhere to be seen.

After Ray landed in the dust, Ronny turned, pushed through the crowd, and walked away. He ignored the taunts of "chicken!" from Raymond's friends. Ronny didn't care. He didn't like to fight and was wet around the eyes from the pain caused by Raymond's blows. There was no way he'd let anyone know he was in that much pain, so he made his way quickly into the school and headed for the bathroom.

The schoolyard reorganized as bus drivers and teachers shouted for everyone to get back in line. The entire confrontation had lasted only a few minutes. Not long enough to attract the immediate attention of principal Dog, who was presumably still in his office. Spy and Rock ran after Ronny and caught up to him just outside the restroom door. They followed him inside.

"Man, Normal, you sure showed Cooley!" said Spy enthusiastically. "I mean, not only did you humiliate him, you threw him into the dirt—at Chuck's feet no less! You should have kicked him!"

Rock shook his head and said, "No. He did the right thing by walking away. It took more guts to do that. Everyone knew that Ronny had won the fight. He didn't need to do anything more. Cooley isn't worth the extra effort."

Rock walked up to where Ronny was examining the bruises he'd have to explain when he got home. He patted Ronny's shoulder and said, "You have class, man. Class!"

The sound of the restroom door opening drew their attention. Chuck Tenant walked in. No one said anything before Chuck did. Chuck smiled. "I heard what Rock just said, and he's right. Walking away made that dweeb look foolish, not you. Everyone's saying good things about you, man."

That broke the tension, and all three of them laughed a little, although Ronny was more than a little embarrassed.

Chuck added, "You should've seen your sister, Normal. Girls crowded around her like a bunch of clucking chickens. They knew you were protecting her."

Ronny was glad to hear that his sister was getting some attention. After all, this was her party.

"Listen," said Chuck. "I know you're a member of Spy's club and all, but I'd like you to feel free to hang with us whenever you want. What do you say?"

Ronny might as well have been invited to hang with a famous rock band by the expressions on Rock and Spy's faces. Ronny had just been invited to spend time with the group of kids considered to be the most untouchable crew around. Everyone called Chuck and his two friends, the "Cool Crew." Ronny just nodded and stammered something like "Thanks" and "Yeah, sure, great." Chuck nodded and then turned around and walked casually out into the hall.

Ronny, Myrna, and Spy biked home together. In his excitement, Spy couldn't help recapping the entire fight until he waved goodbye and split off onto his street. Myrna shouted, "See you tomorrow, Spy!" She turned to Ronny as they swerved to avoid hitting a dead squirrel.

She asked, "Why can't I be in your club?"

Ronny knew this question was inevitable. He looked somewhat sad when he answered her.

"Well, KRSPY would be mean to you, especially now, since you're my kid sister. Besides, you're only a fourth grader. We only accept fifth and sixth graders, and only if we need someone. But, you know all that."

She was disappointed. He could see it in her face. He hated to see her lower lip stick out.

"Look," he said. "I can do this much. If we need someone outside the club for a special assignment, I'll ask Spy to consider you for it. How's that?"

Myrna smiled. "All right!" She agreed, and then shouted, "Race ya to the next street!"

She stood up on her pedals for extra speed, but Ronny wouldn't let her win just because she was his kid sister. He caught up and passed her. They were both out of breath by the next block.

As they neared their home, they could hear birds chirping in the trees. There was the smell of freshly cut grass in the air. The fragrant smoke of backyard burning flavored the air from spring through fall. Leaf burning started in earnest with the end of summer. This time of year, it consisted mainly of debris from several types of deciduous trees. Early spring always foretold its arrival with the heavenly smell of Daphne. That scent was starting to fade, but the fruit trees were beginning to blossom, replacing the Daphne with their sweet aroma.

They rode the last two minutes home in silence. He was in a lot of pain. His ribs, neck, and lower back ached from his fight with Raymond. By the time they arrived and pushed their bikes around into the backyard, Ronny was starting to get stiff.

June, Friday the 13th

March, April, and May passed as school days always do, with some homework, plenty of goofing around, and the usual grumbling over chores around the house. For Ronny, the month of June welcomed graduation from grade school, pending junior high. It also brought an increase in what his parents expected of him by way of yard work. Summer meant lawn care.

Ronny wiped sweat from his forehead. He'd just finished mowing and raking the backyard. He dropped the yard rake and walked over to where he'd set his iced tea down on the picnic table. *Strapping three rakes together might have gotten the job done quicker*, he thought. Earlier today, David Hazelwood, his father, caught him in the garage trying to build a super rake. He laughed and told Ronny that by the time he finished building a giant rake, he could have the yard done with the one he already had. Ronny gave it up, and reluctantly went back to work.

He swallowed the last drop of tea and squinted against the bright glare of the sun. His mother was calling him in for lunch. Perfect timing. He felt starved and was hungry enough to eat a whole package of hot dogs all by himself.

His youngest sister, Jan, ran out the sliding door to meet him. She was holding a piece of paper up for him to inspect.

"See, Ronny! I wrote something for you to print on that thing you got from Grandpa!"

She meant the plastic printing press. He and Myrna had been selling subscriptions to a neighborhood newspaper he set and printed himself. So far, he'd only sold two subscriptions at ten cents a week. The big story in the last issue concerned what

Ronny called the "secret park."

Jan was jumping up and down enthusiastically. "Here," she said, "this is a real story." Ronny could see enough of her scribbling to recognize Jan's pitiful attempt at writing. She was only in second grade.

"Everyone knows about the park," she insisted. "It's no secret, you know. This is a better story." She rushed on with barely a breath. "Why do you call it a secret?"

Ronny hurriedly spoke before she could interrupt. "Because there are secrets in there, that's why."

Jan's eyes grew wide. "What secrets?" she whispered.

At that moment, Clara, his mother, stepped out and repeated her call to lunch. That got him off the hook, for now. He did accept the piece of paper from Jan and ruffled her hair. *Poor kid*, he thought and walked into the house.

Clara reminded Ronny to shut the door behind him and wipe his feet. She told him that a few of his friends had dropped by a half-hour earlier to invite him out for a bike ride. She'd invited them back in a couple of hours after his yard work was finished.

After lunch, Jan tapped Ronny on his arm.

"Ronny?"

"Yeah."

"Toni wants to see you." She grinned. "I think you like her. Too bad, she goes to a private school."

He looked into her soft eyes and recognized a little bit of that female talent to understand matters of the heart, even at her age. Amazing.

"Yeah," he said. "I guess."

Toni lived at the end of the street, four houses down. He did like her quite a bit, and she knew it. She liked him in return. She was cute, with gold colored hair and dimples. He loved her dark brown eyes, but mostly he liked her because she would toss a baseball around with him, which was neat. He occasionally wandered toward her house, hoping to see her at play or watching from her window.

After lunch, David told Ronny that he had a surprise for him and led him out to the front porch. They both enjoyed watching the neighborhood from the front porch, after meals.

David closed the front door behind them. Ronny asked, "Yeah? What is it, Dad?"

David cleared his throat. "Well, Ron, you remember when I said I'd like to take you spelunking someday?"

"Yeah, sure, you mean cave hopping, checking out caves, to help me earn my scout merit badge . . . right?"

David nodded. "That's right." He paused to take note of skinny Mr. Porter in the house, diagonally across the street. He was rolling their family barbecue out of their garage. Mr. Porter spotted David and Ronny and waved. They both waved back, and David continued. "I want to take you around to about four of them this weekend, tomorrow. We'll start with a guided tour of the Oregon Caves, then check out a few lava tube systems on our own. We'll finish with the Wind Cave on Sunday."

Ronny nodded silently, and his father continued. "You can do some work on your merit badge while we're at it. We'll stay somewhere with a pool on Saturday night. What do you say?" Ronny was ecstatic. From Mr. Porter's vantage, Ronny appeared to be bouncing all over the front porch. Mr. Porter cupped his hands around his mouth and shouted, "You must have told him about the cave trip!" David made an exaggerated nod and waved back. Porter laughed and went to work pouring briquettes into his barbecue. Ronny started to run inside to pack up for the big weekend, stopped, and walked back to his father's side. He looked up into his father's inquiring face and then over at Mr. Porter.

"Dad?"

David lifted his eyebrows and followed his son's gaze. Ronny looked back at his father and then at Mr. Porter again. Porter was lighting his grill. Ronny seemed unsure of himself and stammered a little when he said, "I think there's something weird about Mr. Porter."

"Why do you think that?"

"Well, I was over there playing with Lester, while Frank Far . . . I mean Frank wasn't around, and I saw Mr. Porter go into his garage workshop. You know, where he makes fishing flies and stuff. I peeked into the garage and saw him wearing Mrs. Porter's bra."

This was the last thing David expected to hear.

"What?"

Ronny nodded. "Yeah, and Lester says he does it all the time. I asked him about it. Why does Mr. Porter wear Mrs. Porter's bra?"

David smirked. He'd never seen any indication that Porter enjoyed cross-dressing, but then again Ronny didn't know anything like that even existed in this world. There was no reason not to believe him. He looked back at Porter and then down at Ronny's concerned face. He smiled and then abruptly broke out laughing. *Amazing*, he thought, *the things you find out through the innocent eyes of children.*

"Why are you laughing, Dad?"

"Because it sounds so ridiculous that it's probably true, son." David had to give Ronny some explanation, so he said, "He was probably goofing around or something. He'd be embarrassed if he knew you saw him."

"Oh, don't worry. I won't say anything."

With that, Ronny shrugged and went back inside.

Packing for the weekend trip was absorbing all of Ronny's attention when he heard the doorbell and his mom's voice in the hall. His room was close to the front door. There followed a sudden pounding on his bedroom door as though a dozen fists were knocking on it.

He screamed above the noise. "It's unlocked!"

The door flew open, and a flood of kids piled through into his room — ten of them.

"Oh, man!" Eyeball exclaimed. "To be in the inner sanctum of the infamous Ronny Normal. This place is cool!" Eyeball rolled his huge eyes with an appraisal. He did this every time he visited Ronny. He liked acting out his fantasy of being an overly enthusiastic tour guide, so he waved his hands and indicated a large display of space toys in one corner of the room. "Over here," he announced, "you've got your Major Matt Mason collection, complete with moon base and a giant robot." He turned his attention toward another corner and said, "Over there is Normal's card collection, comics, and record player."

Lorraine and Lisa were studying the plastic "Big Press" Ronny had on a table against a wall. They interrupted Eyeball. Lisa said, "Hey, Normal. Is this what you use to make your newspaper?"

Ronny continued to pack his scouting supplies while his friends ransacked his room.

"Yeah," he answered, "that's it. Hey guys, be careful in here, would ya?"

Brain spotted Ronny's walkie-talkies and asked, "Who do you talk to with these?"

"Spy, but they don't work well enough. Too much static." Spy whacked Brain on the arm.

"Who else do you think he talks to on it? No one else lives close enough."

Brain laughed and said, "Maybe that girl down the street, Toni."

Now it was Ronny's turn to cuff Brain, but Brain dodged the blow and offered, "I have an idea for these things. I'll boost their signal if you let me try. I've just gotten a cool schematic I want to try out. What do you guys say?"

Brain looked hopeful, but his answer would have to come later. Ronny ignored him because his model collection was getting a review, and he wanted to hear it.

Jimmy the Spit Goblin, Melvin Tupps the Wad, Pokerface Tim, and Philip the Spy-Guy were all examining Ronny's collection of figure models. They were in awe.

Pokerface spoke in a hushed voice, "Wow. I didn't know you had so many of the Aurora Monster Models!"

Goblin and Wad were more impressed with the models from the new television series, Star Trek. Ronny had the Enterprise, a Phaser, and a Tricorder.

Wad spoke in hushed tones. "Man, I want these."

Spy was turning a couple of models around in his hands. He'd always wanted the NASA spacecraft models but never managed to save up enough money to buy them. He picked up a couple of figure models and remarked, "You've even got both models from The Man from Uncle. Wow!"

Lorraine turned to Ronny and asked the obvious question.

"Where did a kid like you get the money for all this stuff?"

"I guess I just earned it or got them as gifts from my grandfather. I don't know. Why?" Lorraine shrugged.

There were two other kids in the room standing by the door. Rock and Larry Powers. Ronny finished packing his backpack.

He had noticed Larry and how out of place Larry was acting.

"Hey, Powers, I thought you were hanging out with Hawks." Larry looked a little irritated and replied, "Naw. Hawks is a jerk, and his friends stink. I came along because Rock invited me."

That was Rock's cue.

"Larry's OK. Besides, most of us are graduated out of that school now anyway. Including Larry. Lisa, Pokerface, and Eyeball are the only ones in here going back to the Heights next year."

Pokerface turned to Ronny and said, "Yeah, Normal, both spy clubs are all washed up now that you and Spy have graduated. Even Ted Hawks and Sack Heinemann are out. There's no way Alfred the Corpse or Tommy Crotch could ever inspire enough imagination to keep KRSPY going without those two."

They all agreed that the spy clubs were dead. There was some remorse over that. They were at Ronny's place today because they wanted to come up with something to replace their club activities. After spending two years playing spy vs. spy, they felt desperate for another adventure.

Spy-Guy was the leader of a now-defunct spy club, but he didn't lack new ideas. After several of Spy's suggestions, leading invariably to some benign mischief, Brain was the one who came up with the first good idea.

"Hey, I know! Let's ride down to the Dairy Queen. After that, we could take over the park. Everyone's got some money for ice cream, right?"

They all checked their pockets.

"I don't," said Eyeball.

Lisa gave him some change. She smiled.

"Here, Eyeball. You can owe me." Then she walked up and

touched his cheek. "I'm not going to call you Eyeball any more. I never did think your eyes were all *that* big."

Eyeball lowered his eyes with a shy smile. Within a minute, Ronny's room was empty, and he pulled his door shut as they all left through the front door. Ronny had to run around back to get his bike. When he did, he ran into his little sister, Jan. She was lurking behind some bushes. She jumped out and shouted, "Boo!" Without hesitation, she added,

"Can I come too?"

He shook his head. "No, you're not old enough. Besides, you don't have a bike."

Jan cried a little, but Ronny knew it was mostly for show.

Rock and Larry were drinking chocolate shakes with Ronny when a limousine pulled into the small Dairy Queen parking lot. They watched as the driver got out and ordered some ice cream for a young girl about their age that peered out through the limo's back window. Judging by the sad longing on her face, it appeared as though she would rather play. Ronny was so taken with her that he accidentally knocked over his shake. It spilled all over the table. That didn't matter. What did matter was that he'd embarrassed himself in front of that cute little rich girl?

As he looked hopelessly down at the mess on the table, the chauffeur opened the passenger door, leaned in to give the girl her ice cream and then leaned back out to look at Ronny. The little girl had said something to him, and he nodded again. Then the driver walked over to Ronny and asked, "Was that chocolate shake?"

Ronny was stunned that the man was talking to him. He nodded and answered, "Uh, huh."

The chauffeur glanced back at the girl who was now smiling at Ronny out the side window. He surprised Ronny further by saying, "The young lady would like to buy you another of whatever it was that spilled. Would that be all right?"

By now, it seemed as though everyone in the parking lot was staring at Ronny. He was embarrassed but said, "Sure, yeah. Tell her, thanks." The driver nodded and went to get him another shake. The rich girl was smiling and waving to Ronny. He smiled and waved back, then let his eye drift to his friends. Were they were smirking? The show Twilight Zone came to mind. When the driver returned, he brought with him one of the Dairy Queen employees to wipe up the table and hand Ronny his new shake.

After the limo had gone, all of Ronny's friends crowded around him. The guys slapped Ronny on the back, although Ronny noticed something odd in Lorraine and Lisa's eyes. Was it because of the little rich girl's generosity? He wagged his head and thought, *Girls, are weird.*

Something Awful

Early Saturday morning, David Hazelwood already had their yellow Chevy Malibu station wagon packed and ready to leave by the time Ronny finished breakfast. The day promised to be mostly sunny. According to the television weather report, it would cloud up slightly the further south they drove.

It took over three hours to drive from Salem to Grants Pass, and then to Cave Junction. Once they parked at Cave Junction, there was a short hike from the parking lot to the cave entrance. Clara had packed lunches for the day. They ate at the car before gearing up for the cave. The Oregon Cave was the first on David's weekend schedule and the Wind Cave, further East, was the last.

They were dressed warmly and wore hiking boots with rubber soles for traction. The cave would be damp and slippery. Outside, it was around fifty-five degrees. David assured Ronny that it would be much colder in the cave.

They were surrounded by open range. The air smelled of dry ponderosa pine needles, sage, dust, more evergreen trees, and a nearby river. There was the unmistakable smell of decomposing plants and dead fish from a riverbank nearby. He swatted at irritating gnats, mosquitoes, and flies.

The hike to the cave was fascinating in itself for one Boy Scout and his once Explorer Scout father. Ronny had his eyes open for anything that might be useful in his constant quest for achievement awards and merit badges. On the way to the cave, he stopped to look for interesting bugs. The brief trip to the cave mouth ended up taking fifteen minutes.

Star thistle, desert sage, and various wild grasses scented the air. He spotted a couple of western fence lizards, a field mouse, and a few jumping kangaroo mice. The frantic shake of a rattlesnake tail got his immediate attention. Snakes hid under large rocks and behind the scrub brush. Judging by the loud rattle, he had inadvertently come too close to one of them. Ronny thought he spotted the tail of a rattlesnake coiled near the base of a bush very near where he stood. He stepped away from danger then shaded his eyes with a hand while glancing at the treetops. He heard the loud call of blue jays. Birds were another Boy scouting passion. Ronny already had one bird watching achievement badge and was after a similar award. He noted the flat-headed scrub jays, large black crows, red-tailed hawks, and a few solitary turkey vultures flying vigil overhead. From what he knew of this area, he could expect the night to bring owls and bats. Late afternoon would add a chorus of crickets and the chirp of tree frogs.

He continued to poke around rocks, brush, and tree bark. There were several varieties of spiders, including black widows with a venomous bite. He uncovered an alligator lizard and stepped back. They will bite and hold on tenaciously until you drown it under water. He could hear the chirp of grasshoppers everywhere. It was also a good idea to avoid letting any of the local grasshoppers land on your skin because they often bit as well. He thought *It seems like everything out here bites.*

There were too many people around the cave entrance for David's taste, and he told Ronny as much.

"This place is way too touristy for my blood, but it's a good chance for you to get your first taste of spelunking. Real caving might come later." He ruffled Ronny's hair and then surprised him by producing a baseball cap out of his backpack and handing it to his son. Ronny was delighted. It was an old

Cardinals' cap. He didn't know where his father had gotten it.

"Wow! Where did you get this?"

David was about to answer when they were startled by the sudden appearance of a cow wandering nearby. David chuckled and pointed to the cow. He explained that the Bureau of Land Management designated quite a bit of this National Forest as open range. Cattle often wandered into camps and resort areas and had to be chased away.

Ronny forgot his question about the cap and ran over to the cave. He peered around people as they entered. David caught up with him, and they found themselves with a small group of five other people waiting for the tour. There appeared to be plenty of light. Brochures available at the cave entrance explained that white lights for visibility and colored lighting for effects were strung throughout the caves.

Their guide was a young woman with a long brunette French braid. Ronny liked her. She seemed friendly and had adorable freckles. She introduced herself as Natalie. As the tour got underway, Natalie began her running narrative.

"This cave was tailored for tourists. There are distinct paths, bridges, and steps leading up or down." She indicated the ropes strung beside the path. "Please do not to go past these ropes and don't touch any of the formations. Every one of the formations you will see here are extremely old and fragile. The oil from your hands could easily damage or discolor their surfaces."

As she led them deeper into the cave, she pointed out the reddish brown and tan coloration on many of the formations. She explained, "These colors are the result of naturally occurring organic additives."

Natalie changed the subject and drew their attention to the most common formations in the cave system.

"Stalactites are made of calcium carbonate and hang down

from the ceiling like huge calcite icicles. They develop in various sizes and shapes. Stalagmites are spikes of calcite reaching up to the ceiling. They form on the floor of the cave from dripping water."

The soft sound of trickling water drops occasionally punctuated Natalie's narrative.

Ronny thought about the word carbonate. He was reminded of the two compounds he used in his so-called blood sucking juice the stuff he sold at school. One of the liquids was sodium carbonate and water.

Natalie continued her narrative.

"The cave formations are in two categories. Speleogens are erosive features, and Speleothems are mineral deposits consisting mostly of calcite formed by water action."

She mentioned carbon dioxide, carbonic acid, carbonate, and acidic water when describing the erosion factors. Ronny took mental notes on how she described these minerals interacting with each other. He had chemistry projects in mind where this information would come in handy.

David distracted Natalie from her narrative with a question. He pointed to the colored lights hidden behind rocks and formations throughout the considerable length of the cave.

He asked, "Why not stick to white lights? This isn't a haunted house. It's difficult to see everything."

Natalie answered patiently.

"Please forgive the theatrics." She laughed a little and added, "We do intend to entertain as well as inform."

There followed a little knowing laughter from the tourists. The tour rounded a few twists and then ventured up a ladder into a small opening large enough for an adult. Sections with ladders prevented small children from being allowed on tour.

Ronny slid his hands along the ropes. He had no reason to worry about slipping. He knew that one of the state requirements for taking this tour was to wear shoes for adequate traction. Another condition was to provide hard railing wherever it was remotely dangerous.

After a particularly spectacular room, Ronny fought the urge to lag and sneak away from the group. He was a digger and loved scavenging through rock and soil, always as far back as possible. Instead, he reluctantly held on to the ropes.

They passed formations called dome pits, cave scallops, cave ghosts, drop dents, box work, potholes, pendants, and bevels, flowstone, and banded formations that looked like bacon.

She continued,

"Over here, you'll see rocks or grains of material coated with calcite occasionally accumulated in bowl-like depressions on the cave floor like big marbles. These were called cave pearls."

All of these formations glittered under the cave lighting and Natalie's flashlight. Colors included calcite that looked like dirty snow, orange or yellow limonite, and iron-oxide reds. Grays and blacks came from bat guano, manganese, and graphite. There were also greens from impurities of glauconite, potassium iron silicate in layers of dolomite, as well as algae around most of the light sources.

In one of the rooms, Natalie turned out all the lights long enough to see the calcite around them glow. She turned on her flashlight and played it over one formation, then turned it off. The structure glowed slightly.

Natalie explained, "Some rocks glow after exposure to a light source. This is due to certain organic acids that wash into the cave and mix with the crystals found in some of the formations."

When the tour ended, Natalie thanked everyone for coming.

The tourists left the cave through a smaller cave entrance that acted as the exit. The trail around to their vehicles was scenic but failed to provide a topic of discussion that rivaled what they'd seen in the cave.

The rest of that day was spent traveling through the national forests of Central Oregon. They frequently stopped to take pictures and to do some quick exploring. They arrived in Bend by late evening. David said, "Tomorrow we'll get up early and travel out past Prineville to a little town called Post." He tapped the map and indicated Prineville's location on a map Ronny was holding in his lap. "It's just north of the Ochoco National Forest, right here. That's where we'll find the lava tube systems." He pointed out a few more spots on the map. "See, here's the Ice Cave, and the Pictograph Cave, and this one is the Skeleton Cave. Over here is the Hidden Forest Cave. All of these are lava caves. We'll start home Sunday afternoon and take a brief detour down to the Oregon Wind Cave." He tapped the map again. "It's about eighteen miles southeast of Bend." As David promised, they stayed in a nice hotel and spent the rest of Saturday evening lounging around the pool. They both slept well that night. In Ronny's dreams, he explored caves on Mars. Up to this point in his life, his thoughts were saturated with space, caves, and images from school. Ideas about girls were mysterious, but not particularly disturbing. That would change in a little over twenty-four hours.

Sunday, around 1:30 in the afternoon, David pulled into the small dirt parking lot at the Wind Cave. The day was warm but windy. A few clouds drifted in an otherwise blue sky. As the dust settled around the car, they spotted a sign that said, "No littering, alcohol, human waste, campfires, or pets." David explained that this was Forest Service property, so Ronny needed to be careful not to take anything significant from the cave. Apart from the parking lot, there was a path leading to the main entrance. They grabbed their jackets, light packs, and flashlights before David locked the car.

By now, Ronny was good at picking out the local flora and fauna from a distance. It was an open area and easy to make out the lay of the land. He spotted ponderosa pine, juniper trees, and manzanita bushes. Everywhere, the ground was graveled with red lava rocks. Loud solitary crows violated the otherwise peaceful environment with squawks and long-distance quarrels with other crows. Robins appeared interested in the juniper berries, and he spotted a red-tailed hawk soaring high above them.

They didn't speak to each other as they walked the short path leading to the cave entrance. A solitary pine tree loomed to the right of the trail. Ronny wondered at how lonely it appeared. David pointed to the slight grade down to the main entrance. Giant ants crawled nearby, and a small lizard scurried out of sight to hug the shade behind a boulder.

"Watch the rubble, son. You could lose your footing and fall."

The cave entrance was wide and tall enough for two people to enter moving side by side. Ronny followed his father.

David pointed into the dark recesses of the cave and said, "It extends west from the entrance and climbs slightly higher the further in we go. I want to go back as far as possible. We might have to do some climbing over rocks. Are you up to this?"

Ronny looked eager to start.

"Yeah! Let's go!"

Behind them, they could hear the approach of another vehicle. Ronny turned to see what kind of car it was when something bright blinded him for a moment. He blinked and tried to shade his eyes.

David frowned. "You all right, son? What's wrong?"

Ronny looked for the source of the light and found a tin can lid leaning against a rock, reflecting the sun. He pointed to the lid. David nodded, then turned and walked into the cave.

When Ronny moved to follow, he felt as though the air had abruptly changed temperature. The warm air around him chilled suddenly, and he thought he saw his breath. He hurried his steps, entered the cave, and walked next to his father. Now the cold air was gone. What was happening?

"Dad, I just felt some icy air. Weird, creepy, cold air. Did you feel it?"

David shook his head and looked down at Ronny. "No, but it's probably coming from inside the cave. It's a lot cooler in there."

David patted his son on the shoulder.

"Come on."

Ronny didn't follow him right away.

"Dad, I want to look around outside a little. Is that OK with you?"

David shrugged.

"Sure. I suppose so. Look, this cave doesn't go back very far. It only takes a careful twenty to thirty minutes to go as far back as possible. Why don't you scout around outside when we get back?"

Ronny shook his head.

"I don't know. I still feel creeped out. If I wait for a little, maybe the creeps will go away."

David smiled and nodded without pursuing the issue. He shrugged and said, "I'm going to check out that hole I told you about. Come on in when you're ready."

Ronny watched his father walk further into the cave. Then

he wandered around to find the cold spot he'd felt earlier, but the odd chill was gone. There didn't seem to be any trace of it. He stood just inside the cave mouth. The difference between the air outside and inside wasn't different enough to account for what he'd felt.

He stepped out into the sun. In the parking lot, two couples had gotten out of a car and were gathering gear from the trunk. He shrugged his shoulders and instantly felt foolish. He decided to catch up with his father.

From the moment he re-entered the cave he was unaccountably afraid, and he knew something was wrong. Add to that; the cold spot had returned. It surrounded him. His heart started to pound and panic welled in his throat.

A subtle breeze blew through the cave, sounding ominous and frightening. It was as though he had entered the open jaws of a monster. He ran the short distance to where his father stood to stare up at the ceiling. David heard Ronny's approach. He noticed concern on his son's face, but he passed it off as residual "creeps."

David was illuminated by a bright light shining down on him. Ronny thought, *Are there electric lights in here?* As he drew nearer, he saw that sunlight was filtering down through a two-and-a-half-foot-wide hole. Now, Ronny knew how the cave got its name. The wind howled a ghostly lamentation through that hole in the ceiling. It blew in through the cave entrance and out through the hole or the other way around.

Ronny forgot his trepidation for a moment. "Wow, that's awesome!"

David chuckled and responded, "Yeah, well some people like to ignore the main entrance and rappel down into the cave through here. The BLM is going to have to put a fence around that hole. Somebody's going to break a neck."

Ronny remembered his briefly forgotten fear. He frowned and looked at the dark cave around him.

"Dad?"

David put a hand on Ronny's shoulder.

"What's up?"

Ronny continued to watch the shadows.

"I feel like there's something not right in here. Something bad. I want to leave." He indicated the deeper recesses of the cave. "I don't want to go in any further. Can we go home now?"

David was shocked by the sound of fright in his son's voice.

"I don't understand. You can't want to go right now, do you?" He pointed further into the cave and said, "There's bound to be a lot of interesting specimens for you back there."

Ronny grabbed his hand.

"No, Dad. I mean it! Something's wrong about this place."

David studied his son's fearful expression. Ronny let go of his hand and backpedaled away from him toward the main entrance.

"Wait," David implored. "Look, Ron. If you don't come in, then lets at least get a picture of me waving up at you through the hole, and then we'll leave. Maybe you're just burnt out on caves this weekend. I don't blame you."

Ronny shook his head.

"No, it's not that." He stopped backpedaling and said, "I'll take the picture, but then can I wait for you outside?"

David nodded and reassured him with a smile.

The two couples now entered the cave. Ronny could hear them conferring with each other. He thought he heard the names Fred and Ferlin as they spoke to each other. Ronny thought he might have heard the names Glenda and Sharon, but wasn't sure. He was too freaked out to pay much more attention to it.

He could see their flashlights waving over the cave walls. Time seemed to lag as he turned around to leave. His body felt heavy. His throat was tight.

As Ronny prepared to walk around the couples, he ran into another cold spot of icy air. He shivered. Flashlights passed over his face, causing him to blink. He hesitated, and at that moment felt a light hand on his shoulder. He turned around, expecting to see his father looming behind him. There was no one there. David remained standing near the hole, watching Ronny and mystified by his son's behavior. He was nowhere near enough to put a hand on his shoulder. Ronny gulped back his surprise and hurried past the couples. In his mind, he could almost hear his father yelling for him to slow down.

Once away from the cave, he instantly felt better. The terror mysteriously vanished. He could hear the screech of a hawk and the rattling cackle of a crow. The ever-present howl of wind blowing through the cave reminded him that his father was waiting for him to take a picture.

Wiping dust from his nose and mouth, he removed his backpack and lowered it next to his feet. Within a few moments, he had his camera out and was ready to take the picture his father wanted. He hastily tossed the pack over one shoulder and hurried past the lone pine tree to find the hole in the roof of the cave.

Some attempt had been made to erect a fence around the hole. It had been damaged and removed. He looked around and spotted a fence remnant nearby. Without a fence around it, this was a dangerous place to be standing. Dropping his pack, he peered down into the hole. There was his dad waving and smiling up at him. Ronny waved back and wasted no time in snapping the picture. When he lowered the camera, he noticed something strange next to his father; some disturbance like a heat wave. He rubbed his eyes. When he peered back down through the hole, it was gone.

His father saw the confusion on his son's face. He called up to him.

"What is it, son?"

Ronny already felt embarrassed, so he said, "Nothing, Dad. Hurry, OK?"

David nodded and stepped out of the light.

Ronny grabbed his pack and decided to sit on the ground with his back against the pine tree.

What happened in there? He let his mind wander. He pondered the idea that perhaps his father was right. They might have visited too many caves for one weekend. That must be it. That thought made him feel better. He pulled a bag of beef jerky out and tore it open with his teeth. By the time he was halfway through his first piece, he temporarily forgot his unexplained fears.

On the far side of the parking lot from where he sat, two chipmunks ran along the ground and chased each other through some brush. Ronny swatted at the occasional fly while listening to the ever-present drone of insects. Occasionally, he spotted a dragonfly and heard the hum of its wings. He batted at what he thought was a fly on his neck and then realized it was an ant. Looking around at where he sat, he discovered an anthill several feet away.

"Great," he muttered, then got up and dusted himself off. Several more ants were crawling on his legs. He brushed them off, then grabbed his pack and wandered over to the station wagon. The door was locked, so he threw his backpack onto the roof. The idea of waiting beside the car didn't appeal to him at all. What was keeping his father?

While he waited, he opened his pack and inspected some

of the rock specimens he'd managed to pick up without any objections from his father. Although taking samples was not allowed on government property, what they didn't know wouldn't concern them.

As he studied his collection, he heard the approach of another vehicle; a Volkswagen van. He watched the vehicle as it parked and people climbed out. It contained a load of Boy Scouts in shorts and short-sleeve uniforms. He surmised that they were on an official field trip. He contemplated an urge to walk over and get to know this group, then noticed that they were Explorer scouts. They were way out of his league, for now.

He glanced over his shoulder just as his father emerged from the cave. Ronny walked over to him.

"Hey, Dad, you didn't feel anything weird in there?" David shook his head.

"It's just a cave, son. Maybe what you felt was meant for you alone." He smiled and tousled Ronny's hair.

Ronny knew his father was trying to make him feel better and not embarrassed. Instead, it had the reverse effect. He pondered the statement his father had just made. Was his father right about that? Was the feeling meant for him alone? Worse yet, that hand on his shoulder. There was something awful in there. Was it something interested solely in him? He shuddered at the thought.

The drive home was quiet. They stopped at a rest area and then a little later for hamburgers. After eating, Ronny slept in short naps most of the way home. During these naps, he had strange dreams. The dreams he remembered were about a beautiful but sad ballerina. Sometimes she was dressed in pink, but usually in black or dark purple. She pirouetted and circled toward him, then cried and begged for help. She said that someone had killed her. In the first dream, she was blurry, yet in successive dreams, she became easier to see., In the last dream before arriving at home, the ballerina screamed and reached out to him. As he stretched out his hand to her, he was suddenly frightened by the sudden appearance of a man wearing a ski mask and carrying a large hammer. Ronny was shocked when the man swung the hammer and bludgeoned her on the side of her head. She fell bleeding and dying onto a featureless gray floor. Ronny followed her fall with his dreamy eyes. When he looked up again, her attacker had disappeared.

Secrets

Ronny awakened suddenly. He bolted upright in the backseat as they turned the corner and entered their driveway. His dream of the ballerina was fresh in his mind. How could he forget it? She'd nearly touched him just before the vision of her violent death. He'd never seen anything like that on television, not even close. Monster movies included. A sudden chill swept over him. He expected it to intensify into what he had felt in the cave. Thankfully, it didn't, although gooseflesh crept down his back and arms.

David saw him awaken through the rearview mirror.

"Hey, buddy, we're home." He noticed Ronny's ragged expression and remarked, "You look rough. Don't tell me you just got slapped in your dream for stealing a kiss from the little girl down the road. What is her name?"

"Toni."

David replied, "Yeah, Toni."

When Ronny didn't appear interested in the topic, David changed it.

"Hey, it's dinner time, champ. Let's see if your mother has something ready. If not, we can fix something ourselves."

David was about to jump out of the car when Ronny stopped him.

"Hey, Dad. Before we go in can, I ask you something?"

"Sure. What's up?"

There was a pause. Ronny appeared lost in thought. David frowned and studied his son's face for clues as to what was wrong and then asked, "What's bothering you, Ron?"

Ronny took a deep breath and told his father everything, including the rest of what he'd experienced at the Wind Cave and the dreams he'd had on the way home.

David listened with interest then said, "It was probably bad dreams caused by your emotions at the cave. That's all. Nothing to worry about, son."

Ronny waited for his father to announce something about going to bed early tonight, but he didn't. Instead, David just said, "Let's try not to mention anything about this to your mom right now. She wouldn't like it, and she couldn't do anything about it anyway. You and I will sort this out. OK?" A thought occurred to David. "Why don't you ride down the street after dinner and see if Toni is outside. It'll take your mind off of this for a while, but don't steal a kiss unless you're ready for her reaction."

Ronny blushed, grabbed his pack, and said, "OK."

Clara was in bed with a headache. Jan and Myrna had made dinner. It consisted of macaroni and cheese. Jan had little to do with it apart from contributing to the mess. David examined the results of their efforts with evident compassion for a job well conceived but radically overproduced. When comparing the fruits of their labor to the mess they left behind, Thanksgiving supper would have been expected and not a small bowl of macaroni and cheese. Nevertheless, their little faces were aglow with pride.

Jan grabbed the sticky serving bowl and held it up for inspection.

"Dad!" Jan yelped with enthusiasm. "We made dinner for Mom. See?"

David and Ronny stifled a laugh, but Myrna heard it and became angry. She said, "Don't you dare laugh. We worked hard on this."

Jan lowered the macaroni bowl and looked pitiful. David spared them all any embarrassment.

"It looks great," he said, "but . . . I don't think there's enough. Let's make something else to go with it." Before any of them could offer to help, he added, "I'll take care of it and call you when it's ready."

He noted his daughters' powdered cheese-covered hands and faces and then Ronny's dust-covered body and groaned while wrinkling his brow.

"All of you better go and wash up."

Ronny took this opportunity to unload the rest of the car and hefted his father's pack out of the back of the station wagon. He was startled by a soft girl's voice behind him.

"Hello."

He turned around. It was Toni.

"Hi," was all that choked out of him.

Neither of them was unusually shy. The moment merely seemed awkward. He lowered the pack onto the open tailgate and cleared his throat. *Here she is*, he thought. *I'd better not mess up.*

"Hey, Toni . . . . I'm supposed to eat pretty soon. Are you going to be out here for a while? We could ride up to the park or something."

She smiled.

"Sure. I'll be in my backyard. Come over and yell over the gate. I'll let you in."

With that, she waved and walked away. Ronny smiled and waved back, then picked up the pack again and took it inside.

After dinner, he helped to gather the dishes and then quickly left for Toni's house.

Clara stopped him at the front door.

"It'll be dark in about an hour. Make sure you're back by then."

"Yeah, Mom. No problem."

He parked his bike in front of Toni's garage. He'd never met her parents, so he had no way of knowing if they would get mad at him for leaving his bike there. Crossing his fingers, he glanced around the right side of the garage to see if anyone was watching through the open blinds. No one was there. He walked around the left side of the garage and grabbed hold of the top of the old wooden fence. Pulling himself up, he peeked over the fence into the backyard. Where was she? He saw the tall evergreen trees that bordered all of the homes on this side of the street. They were swaying slightly in a light breeze. Those trees belonged to the park he referred to as the "secret park." He'd always hinted at something dark and scary lurking in those treetops. Ronny had a way of injecting mystery into just about everything.

"Boo!"

He immediately let go of the fence, landed on his feet and spun around. Toni was standing behind him and laughing. He laughed with her.

"Well," he said, "you almost scared me." There was a mischievous glint in her eye.

"Really? Almost? What does it take to scare Ronny Normal?"

He cocked his head to one side and took on a severe expression.

"Something horrifying happened to me today." He could see that excited her, so he pressed on. "You know, I'll tell you about it if you want. But it might frighten you. Do you get nightmares easily?"

She was wide-eyed with interest.

"No . . . I mean, well, sometimes I get them, but tell me anyway."

Ronny took the opportunity for a little theatrics. He glanced around as though he were looking for spies, or worse. He crept past her and stole a look down the street then waved her over to him.

"Where's your bike?" he asked in hushed tones.

She pointed at her back yard. He urged her to get it.

"Hurry. Get it and follow me to the secret park. I'll tell you about it only when I know we're safe from prying eyes."

She was practically breathless.

"OK, I'll hurry."

Ronny winked at her and then nodded toward the gate.

Toni opened the gate by pulling on a cord that released the latch on the other side. Once open, she hurried through. He could hear the swish of her feet running through the grass. While he waited, he glanced back over his shoulder---and then froze. He saw someone standing across the street, staring at him.

It was a middle-aged woman, wearing a loosely fitted gown or housedress. If that wasn't enough, she flickered and changed for a fleeting second into a younger woman wearing a dark ballerina's dress and then vanished as though they were never there.

Ronny rubbed his eyes. Frightened, he voiced a startled sound and turned around to run through Toni's gate. He ran right into Toni, knocking over both her and her bike. She fell, and he landed on top of her. She giggled.

"Now you have to kiss me," she said with a coy lilt in her voice. He was embarrassed and quickly stood brushing himself off while she continued to giggle. He helped her up.

"I'm sorry."

"That's all right. Spy tried to steal a kiss that way once. I guess you weren't trying to do that, huh?"

Spy, Phillip, was interested in Toni? Ronny frowned.

"What?" he asked. "Spy likes you?"

She looked down at her feet and replied, "Yeah, but I don't like him." She looked up and smiled. "I like you."

She moved so deftly that he barely realized she had kissed him on the cheek until it was all over. His face reddened. This was a beautiful and terrifying week for him. First, a rich girl buys him a shake, then a cave gives him the creeps, and he sees a ghost on his street. It had to be a ghost, he thought. Now the girl he has a crush on kisses him. Unbelievable. Regardless, all he could think about at that moment was the ghost across the street. Who was she? Then it hit him. She looked a little like the woman in his nightmares.

He sputtered before he somehow made a fool of himself.

"Hey, Toni, maybe we should do this tomorrow. It's getting kind of late, and Mom wants me back before dark."

She picked up her bike.

"No way. You got me all interested and stuff. Come on. We can hurry."

With that, she stood up on her pedals and pushed down for speed as she wheeled out into the street. Ronny ran around to his bike and joined her. He took the lead as they rode past five homes before turning right. Porter's house was now on their left. Cars were seldom a problem at the entrance to the secret park because the street that they'd turned onto ended within two blocks at a yellow and black striped barrier—a dead-end. At the fence, they turned right and rode into the woods over a narrow dirt path.

One of the many reasons Ronny referred to this as the "secret park" was because the path looked so poorly maintained and forgotten. This wasn't the main entrance. People living on this side of the park had forged the footpath to gain access to it through the woods. At path's end, it opened into a large, well-cared-for city park.

Trees blocked the path on both sides. It was so dense with trees and brush that they could have walked their bikes into them and be completely hidden. The trail took several turns so that they couldn't see the park right away. When they reached the park, they burst into it like the Hansel and Gretel escape from the witch's forest.

As usual, the place seemed deserted. Another reason Ronny called the area a "secret." Someone had spent a lot of money on all the typical playground equipment, plus a basketball court and softball diamond, and yet no one seemed to come here except a few adults now and then. Ronny's father said it was because many of the families who used to live on the first entrance side of the park had moved away. The people that moved into the neighborhood after they were mostly retired. No kids.

Ronny yelled for Toni to follow him. He led the way past the swings to the opposite side of the park where he had cleared a path through some tall blackberry bushes. The trail was high and wide enough to get their bikes through to a place where he thought only he and his friends ever hung out. There was a clearing about ten feet wide. They couldn't see anything over the tops of the blackberry bushes, except the trees towering into a darkening sky. Toni was in awe.

"Wow." She breathed. "I've been to this park lots of times. How come I never found this place?" She looked at him. "This is cool."

He shrugged. "I . . . I don't know. I guess it's OK. Too small."

They leaned their bikes against some vines and sat down on the dry ground. It was darker in here, so he felt a little more urgency to tell her what he'd promised to say to her and then get home before he got into trouble.

She leaned back against her arms with her legs outstretched and crossed her ankles. "OK, go ahead; tell me."

He took a deep breath and repeated the story of what happened at the Wind Cave. When he'd finished, she looked disappointed.

"Is that all?" she asked. "What about the picture you said you took of your dad through the hole? Do you think there was a ghost down there with him? I can't wait until you get the pictures back."

Ronny was amazed.

"What do you mean is that all?" She leaned forward.

"Well, nothing happened. Did it? I mean, nobody was killed or hurt or anything."

OK, he thought. *Here goes nothing.* Since Toni wanted more, he told her about the dreams he'd had, and then told her about the ghost that he thought he saw across from her house. That part *did* get to her. She was shocked and suddenly frightened. He wondered if he shouldn't have told her about the ghost. He felt bad.

Toni seemed terrified.

"A ghost followed you home and was standing across from my house?" she exclaimed.

He tried to calm her down.

"No, take it easy. I didn't say she followed me home. Besides, the ghost was probably just my imagination."

He didn't believe that for a minute, and neither did she. She stood up and put her hands on her hips.

"You're just saying that so I won't be scared. You probably think I'll hug you and ask you to protect me or something. Spy would do that. Don't *you* do it."

She got up off the ground, grabbed her bike, and pushed it back out into the park proper. Ronny got up and followed her with his bike. She jumped onto her bicycle and hurried away with pedals spinning. He did the same. Was she mad at him or just afraid to be out after dark?

"Hey, Toni!" he yelled. "Are you mad at me?"

She turned her head to look at him just as they entered the trees and the footpath on their side of the park. She yelled back, "No, silly! I want to see if the ghost is still there!"

They rode their bikes back to where he saw the ghost. For all of Toni's defiance, the shock and excitement was wearing off. The realization that Ronny had just seen a ghost across the street from her own house was starting to scare her. She looked around and then back at Ronny. She spoke in hushed tones.

"Do you think she's friendly?"

He'd been creeped out ever since he'd seen the ghost woman, so he cut the tough stuff and leveled with her.

"Yeah, I believe she is. I don't know why, but I do. I hope the man in my dream isn't a ghost too. He was scary."

Toni wanted to hear more about that part of Ronny's dream, so he told her all that he remembered about the man. If Toni wasn't on the verge of terror before, she was now. After he finished describing what little he saw of the man, the hammer, and his striking the woman with it, Toni spoke almost breathlessly.

She said, "Do you think he killed her?"

That night Ronny decided to turn out the lights in his room and go to bed early. He was tired, and although he was worried about ghosts and dreams, he felt he was sleepy enough to ignore it. He grabbed his walkie-talkie and beeped Spy. He jumped into bed and tented the covers over his head. He had a flashlight next to his bed, which he pulled under the covers and switched on. Brain had indeed built a signal booster for Spy-Guy and Ronny from parts he'd picked up at an electronics supply. He installed it at Spy's house the weekend Ronny was in Eastern Oregon with his father.

Ronny thought, OK, Brain, let's see if this works. He pushed a button that should beep to alert Spy at the other end. He waited. Nothing. How was this supposed to work if Spy had a booster and he didn't? Brain had explained that the booster would stay on at all times using minimal electric current. It would scan for Ronny's signal and enhance it at Spy's end, then boost Spy's signal at his end so Ronny would have no trouble picking up his voice. Or something like that. According to the Brain, it was "really slick." Well, that remained to be seen.

Just when he thought he would have to give up, Spy-Guy answered his page.

"Normal, is that you? Over."

"Yeah. But forget the 'over' stuff. We don't need it. I can hear the button click as well as you can."

"All right by me," Spy replied.

Ronny said, "I guess you get to pay Brain back for the parts he bought. Remember, you bet him the parts if he could build a booster that worked."

"I remember. Hey, I'm not going to stiff him. You know that." Spy changed the subject. "Did you see anything cool at the caves?"

Ronny spent the next fifteen minutes describing the weekend. He also told him about his dreams and the ghost. He mentioned that she kept asking for help. Spy was impressed and excited.

"Get outta here, Normal! Are you shitting me? A for-real ghost? It sounds like she's going to haunt you forever until you find out what help she wants! Are you going to try to find out? We've got to get the club together and figure this out!"

Ronny couldn't speak until Spy let up on the button on his end. Spy rambled about Rock's new friend, Larry Powers, from Bend. Finally, Spy let go of the button. Ronny was angry.

"Don't do that again, Spy. Give me a chance to talk. Will you?"

He took his finger off the button to let him respond.

"Sorry . . . but maybe Larry's dad could help us."

"Us? Help us with what?" Before Spy could answer, he said, "Oh no, you don't. I know what you're thinking, and you're crazy if you think I'm going back to Bend because of this. And I wouldn't be taking you guys with me if I did. What good would it do? The ghost is here anyway if she's here at all. I might be crazy. Have you thought of that? It's not as if you haven't accused me of being nuts before. Remember when I said I saw a striptease party at a KRSPY meeting while looking through Hawk's clubhouse window? I lied about that. Besides, how would we get to Bend, ride our bikes? Dad's not going to take me back there for something like this. Not in a million years!"

There was a long pause, and then Spy spoke in hurt tones.

He said, "You lied about the striptease?"

Ronny realized that the only thing Spy had heard the part about the striptease.

"Of course, I lied. Do you think that for one second Greg the Sack would have let his girlfriend do a bump and grind for Hawks? Huh? Besides, it's not like Lips looks anything like Chas' cousin. Man, Spy! Come on; you must have guessed I was pulling your leg. Right?"

There was another long pause. Spy didn't say anything, so Ronny did.

"Look, forget about that, and let's get back to the point."

Spy answered in a deadpan voice. "OK. Fine."

Ronny rolled his eyes.

"The second thing is . . . what makes you think a spy club and a guy from Bend can help me with a ghost?"

"Well, I don't know," Spy answered. "Eyeball is pretty good at figuring out weird stuff like that. Remember when that frog kept following his neighbor lady around whenever she worked in her yard? That was Mrs. Fletcher. Eyeball figured that it was because the frog liked her smelly rose perfume."

"It did not."

"Did too. You've heard about this. Don't act as if I'm the crazy one. Eyeball asked Mrs. Fletcher for a little bit of her smelly perfume. He put it on his arm, and the little fellow followed him all the way home. I swear."

"It did not."

"Did too," Spy insisted.

"Spy, this isn't getting us anywhere, so fine, have it your way. If you want to have a secret meeting, it's OK by me . . . but stupid."

"It's settled then." Spy sounded satisfied. "I'll call you tomorrow. I don't think anyone's parents are planning any trips this week so everyone should be able to come. I'll have Rock bring a machete so we can enlarge the hideout in the secret park. My club, my rules."

Ronny wasn't enthusiastic, but he was glad that Spy believed him about the ghost. He said, "Chopping out some more room is a good idea. I took Toni over there tonight, and it does look like it's . . ." Ronny realized his mistake too late. He shouldn't have mentioned Toni to a possible rival, especially since she wasn't part of the more or less defunct spy club. His words grew softer; "it's growing over again."

"You . . . you what?" Spy stammered. "Why did you take Toni into the clearing?"

Ronny thought, *Well, here it comes*. Spy continued before Ronny could explain.

"I get it. You LIKE her and took her out there to do kissy stuff. Don't deny it! Bad move, Normal. Wait till I tell everyone."

Finally, Ronny got his word in. "I don't care what you do. The spy stuff is over anyway. Besides, drunks hang out in there now. I saw more beer bottles and junk. Who cares if she knows? As for kissy stuff, she told me about how you like her and how you tried to kiss her yourself! So, you can knock it off and mind your own business."

More silence. That was how you knew you had Spy where you wanted him. He shut up. Ronny let the silence trail until Spy answered. "Normal? You still there?"

"Yeah."

"All right, fine. Why don't you bring her along to the meeting? Might as well."

"OK, I will," Ronny replied.

Spy said, "I'll call you tomorrow then."

Ronny hesitated before responding. "Yeah, I know. That's what you said."

Spy responded as though he'd already forgotten their quarrel over Toni. "OK, good, sure, then I'll see you tomorrow."

The flashlight was too bright for Ronny's feelings. He turned it off and tossed it unceremoniously out of bed. It hit the floor with a thud. Under normal circumstances, this fight with Spy would have bothered him enough to keep him awake most of the night, but not tonight. He was exhausted.

The walkie-talkie stayed under the covers with him just in case Spy wanted to call and apologize for being a jerk. Right? Fat chance of that.

He closed his eyes and let his mind drift. Mostly, he thought about Toni. Within a few minutes, he was asleep and dreaming. His dream imagery shifted from Toni to the ghost woman. She remained a ballerina rather than the older lady he'd seen briefly across from Toni's place. Ronny noted for the first time that she was a small woman. She danced alone on a darkly lit stage with Ronny as the only apparent spectator in the audience. Her costume was black with what appeared to be tiny pink flowers embroidered throughout the drape-like purple fringe of her tutu. Her hair was shoulder length and loose, and that combined with her pale skin and sad expression gave her an overall air of tragic beauty. Her black toe shoes laced up around her ankles with a shimmer of silk and then blended into black leotards. Her arms, hands, and shoulders moved like the petals of a flower on the surface of the water.

There was a conspicuous lack of music. She performed gracefully to the swish of her legs, the tap of her toes, and loud silence.

Ronny glanced around, looking for the killer he'd seen in his previous dream. He could barely make out the rest of the auditorium. Black draperies hung down from a ceiling so high it was impossible to make out any of the ceiling detail. All around him, the seats were dark. If the killer were hiding in the auditorium, there would have been no way for Ronny to know it. All of the available light came from floodlights above the stage, hidden amongst the ropes and layers of raised backdrops. Ethereal lighting effects followed her every move.

At some indeterminate moment, she stopped dancing.

She finished her last moves with a flourish and bowed to her audience of one. For some reason Ronny felt he should clap, so he did. Who is to say what motivates anyone in dreams? The woman smiled at him, then the lights dimmed, and she ran off-stage to her left.

Ronny turned his head for another look around and found her sitting in the seat directly behind him. His young heart skipped a beat. "Man!" He gasped. "You scared me."

She looked apologetic. "I'm sorry." She considered a moment before adding, "I need to talk with you, Ronny."

A moment later they were standing together on the dimmed stage. In his dream state, Ronny didn't question this abrupt change of location. Instead, he found himself more interested in the woman. For the first time, he could see her. She was not much taller than he was; around five feet or so. Her make-up was heavy, dark, and exotically attractive over pale and petite facial features. Raven black hair hung in rivers by the sides of her face.

Under the circumstances, Ronny didn't know what to do with himself. He struggled for something to say.

"Um . . . aren't you supposed to have your hair pulled back or something?" *Geez*, he thought. *That was a lame question.*

She smiled and replied, "I like it in my face when I feel sad."

"Oh." He gulped.

"Ronny, I'm going to explain why I'm here. I assume you want me to do that."

He nodded, now feeling more than a little anxious. She saw this in his frown.

"You don't have to be afraid. It's straightforward. I've been trying to get someone's attention at the cave for three months. No one was sensitive enough to notice my presence until you came along."

Ronny found his voice. "How did you follow me, home?"

She said, "Your spirit left a bright trail for me. Time and distance are not issues here." She paused a moment. Ronny was listening, so she continued.

"I fear that my son, Thomas, killed me, but I don't know for sure. My killer was wearing a mask and never spoke. I need someone to help me discover the truth. If Thomas was my murderer, I must know why." She noted Ronny's skeptical expression and added, "Do not presume that I know everything just because I crossed over and now exist within a different set of dimensions than you do. Breathing folk imagine that we understand more about the human mind after we pass on as if we can read minds. Why do people assume that?"

Ronny's frown deepened. He asked, "What difference does it make to you now?"

She explained, "In my heart, I don't believe Thomas is responsible for my death. I need to know the truth. Then I can rest. Who is to say what motivates those that cross over?

I am dead to your world, and yet I do want the answer to that question. We feel more deeply in this place by comparison to the way we felt in breathing life. Our needs, passions, and curiosity are keener here than ever before in physical life. I believe the solution to my murder will bring an end to something far worse than my death alone."

Ronny's face reflected his confusion. "What do you mean?"

"Others may follow me. I mean, others may be murdered by this man, whoever he is."

The sudden realization of what she had just said carried terrifying implications. The murderer was alive and quite possibly stalking other prey.

Ronny felt himself tremble. "What do you want me to do? I'm just a kid."

The ballerina suddenly changed from an attractive young woman to a middle-aged lady dressed in a housedress. He'd seen this same appearance across from Toni's house. Without the makeup, she didn't look all that different compared to her younger self. She had a few smile lines, gray in her hair, and she was a little heavier in her build, but apart from that, she looked about the same.

She wouldn't answer him immediately. Instead, she turned and walked away from him to the edge of the stage, then looked out over the darkened rows of seating as though expecting to find someone else watching her. He noticed that she walked with a limp. She looked down at her legs, inspecting them, then shook her head as if to say *no* and continued walking without a limp. Finally, she turned to look back at Ronny. She lifted her hands as if in resignation. "As I've said, I can't get anyone else's attention. Will you help me to at least discover if it was my son, or not, please?"

Ronny was flabbergasted. "How? I'm a little older than some of my friends, but, still, no one listens to a 13-year-old kid."

She answered, "I will help you whenever and however I can. My abilities are limited, but I will do everything in my power to aid you. You may not always see me, but I will not be far from you."

Before he could respond, he heard a loud, intrusive noise that drove everything else out of his mind. It was the clamor of angry birds, fighting.

Ronny awoke with a start.

The summer had proven to be warm, and at times, hot. He wore only his underwear to bed and kept the windows open a crack to allow the cold air into his room. Two robins were fighting in the juniper tree just outside his open window. He jumped out of bed and shut the window, then stood there for a while to think. Could he reconstruct his dream before it faded away?

Ronny pulled on his jeans and walked over to grab some blank paper from the paper-tray side of his "Big Press" toy printer. He sought out a pencil from his desk. Muttering some of the details from the dream aloud, he soon managed to jot down enough detail to help him remember most of the dream. Real or not, his young mind would not dismiss the possibility that it was genuine and that the woman wanted his help. He stepped into the slippers his grandfather had given him last Christmas and put on a blue bathrobe. Looking out the window up at the sky, he found it was a little cloudy. That was likely to burn off quickly according to the local forecast.

Breakfast was a high priority, although he wanted to grab something out of the garage first before he forgot about it. He quietly made his way through the family room, the kitchen, and into the laundry room. The laundry room door led to the garage. He'd barely turned the knob before he heard little slippered feet shuffling through the kitchen and heading his way. His sister, Jan, walked in. She rubbed the sleep from her eyes with her tiny fists.

"What are you doing?" she asked.

He knew there was no chance of stopping her from following him to the garage. Instead of trying to get rid of her, he waved her over. Immediately, she was wide awake. He opened the door then stepped out into the fresh air. Jan followed.

David never parked in the garage. Although it was a two-car garage, there just wasn't room for a car. As Ronny entered, he noted the window on the far left wall, under which was an extended workbench. The workbench nearly covered the entire length of that wall. Shelves and a pegboard above it were loaded with his father's hand and electric woodworking tools. His eyes briefly passed over the rest of the contents of the garage. There were tools for working on the car, a gas can, lawn mower, and boxes left unpacked from their move to Salem Heights three years ago. On his immediate left was another bench covered with Ronny's stuff.

He moved in front of what his father called Ronny's mad scientist workshop. Shelves and another pegboard were hung above the bench just like David's much larger bench. That was where the comparison ended. Viewing Ronny's bench from left to right, the first item to catch his eye was a chemistry set. His father gave it to him when he was in fifth grade. It came in a large carrying case that unfolded into what looked like a mini-laboratory. It opened in three panels with fold-down racks full of chemicals, beakers, litmus paper, and an apparatus for holding things during an experiment. David let him customize it by taking him to a hobby store to buy a Bunsen burner, which he could only use when his parents were home.

The chemicals he used for his infamous blood-sucking juice were in a rack next to the Bunsen burner. First, he mixed sodium carbonate with water and filled six cheap vials with that solution. Next, he half-filled another six vials with a liquid called cresol phthalein. The blood-sucking effect required less of it than the sodium carbonate, so he sold only a half test tube, vial, of it to his customers. Initially, he'd considered using a cheaper chemical called phenolphthalein, but its effect when mixed with the sodium carbonate was more strawberry in color, and he wanted a blood red. After filling the vials, he corked them firmly and taped them together in sets of two vials each.

Jan noticed that Ronny had his blood-sucking stuff lined up and ready to be taped together for sale. She begged Ronny to put some on her. "Please, oh please, oh please. Do it again!"

He quieted her by answering, "Sure," then told her to put her arm out for him.

"Now, hold your arm very still."

Jan's eyes were wide in rapt attention. She held her arm with her other hand so she would remain as still as possible. Ronny held a vial over her arm and said, "First, I put a bead of this sodium carbonate on your arm . . . there."

She reached to smooth it out. He stopped her. "No, don't do that," he said. "Leave it like a big bubble so we can watch the little red bubbles grow inside it." He took a vial of cresolphthalein and let a drop of it fall into the first bubble.

"Here . . . OK . . . now, watch."

He helped her steady her arm while they observed the harmless chemical reaction. Sure enough, tiny red bubbles began to form within the clear liquid. What everyone found to be "cool" about it was that the red bubbles were denser than the surrounding fluid, so they formed on the skin in globules. The apparent effect gave the trick its name. It did look like it was sucking the blood out of Jan's small arm. She was always amazed whenever he would do this for her.

"Wow." She looked up at him and asked, "Can I smoosh it around now?"

Ronny laughed. "Sure, I don't care. You should wash it off your arm afterward, so it doesn't stain something."

"OK," she exulted and then rubbed a finger into the blood-red bubble.

Ronny thought Jan would be satisfied for a while. Not so. She always wanted to smell the chemicals in his lab. It was somewhat weird, but his youngest kid sister was that way. Today, he let her play with a piece of litmus paper. She sniffed at it and made a sour face. Its chemical smell wasn't unpleasant. She always made that face when she sniffed something she thought was 'icky.' He told her to take it outside and put her hand on it under the sun. He explained that if she did that, then the sun would leave a handprint on the paper. This effectively sent her on her way, leaving him to browse his workbench uninterrupted.

His eyes moved on from his chemistry set to the middle of his bench. There was his "Incredible Edible" set for making chewy, edible bugs. Next to that was a device with several molds for making little plastic toys. Lastly, there was his elaborate set of tools, paints, and props for customizing his model collection.

He turned his attention to an object tucked away in a cubbyhole above his edible bug machine. This was what he'd come into the garage to get. It was six inches long, an inch wide and carefully wrapped in tinfoil. He removed the foil, exposing a dark stick of wood engraved with bold Central American designs. Chas gave this to him. It was supposed to be imbued with magical properties or something like that. He had ignored it and stashed it away because he had no idea what to do with it. It was time to visit Chas if he wasn't still grounded for playing peeping Tom on his cousin Lacey last week.

Ronny shoved the stick into his back pocket and ran into the kitchen. *Oh yeah*, he thought. *Food*. He opened the cupboard to take out his favorite cereal, Corn Flakes and then grabbed milk out of the refrigerator.

Just then, the telephone rang.

He waited for his parents to pick up the phone. When it was apparent that they had, he finished making breakfast and sat down to the table to eat. Midway through his second bite, his father came out of the bedroom, excited about something.

"Ron, its Phillip. He's still on the line."

"It's Spy, Dad. He likes to be called Spy." Then Ronny noticed confusion in his father's expression, and not about Phillip's nickname.

"What . . . What is it, Dad? You look weirded out?"

Rather than answering him, David quickly walked to the kitchen telephone hanging on the wall. He picked it up and spoke to Phillip before handing it to Ronny.

"Here, Phil, you tell him about it yourself."

Ronny accepted the handset and watched his father walk back down the hall to his bedroom and turn on the radio in his bedroom. Ronny could hear his father tuning in the local news station.

"Hey, Spy. What's up?"

Spy-Guy was practically out of breath.

"Man, Normal, you're not going to believe this! My dad and I were listening to the news on the radio, waiting for the weather, when a report said two guys found a dead woman at the back of the Oregon Wind Cave!" There was a breathy pause, followed by, "Well, can you believe *that*?"

Ronny was suddenly as excited as Spy.

"No kidding? When and how far back into the cave did they find her?"

Spy said, "She was killed and then buried at the cave. They found her the same day you and your dad were there on Sunday!"

"Come on, Spy. Where did they find the body? How far back in the cave was she found?"

"I don't know. The news will probably come back on in a while. Police are still looking for the killer."

David stepped out of his bedroom. "Hey, son. They're repeating the story on the news right now."

Ronny nodded.

"Got to go, Spy. I'll call you back."

He hung up the phone without waiting for a reply and then ran into his parents' bedroom. His mother was up and dressed in a robe. She was listening for the report. It seemed that this news was a hot topic. When they were all seated on the bed, the news broadcast reported what they were waiting to hear. The gist of the story stated that a fifty-five-year-old woman by the name Beverly Winston had been killed. Her body was found last Sunday at the Wind Cave, southeast of Bend. She was buried just outside a small opening into the cave. Two men, one named Fred and the other Ferlin, had found the body after exploring an opening at its northeastern end much smaller than the main entrance. When interviewed, Fred claimed the flies were what gave away the fact that something was amiss. At first, they thought that perhaps some deer had been poached and the remains had been buried nearby. When they crawled through the opening, into the sunlight, they dug around until they found the body later to be identified as the widow, Mrs. Winston. She'd been missing from her home for three months."

Ronny was stunned. He remembered the names he'd heard spoken behind him as he backed out of the cave; Fred, Ferlin, Glenda, and Sharon. In horror, it occurred to him that most likely he would have found the body himself if he and his father had continued into the cave. Ronny was a digger, with an eager abundance of fact-finding curiosity to match.

When the report was over, Clara and David looked at their son. Ronny's face had turned pale. He was staring at the radio as though he fully expected it to come to life, leap off the dresser, and then chase him around the room. David touched him on the arm. Ronny jumped.

David said, "That must have been what you sensed at the

cave and why you wouldn't go in. We would have found her. Is that what you're thinking?"

"Yeah," Ronny replied as though dazed. Then he seemed to snap out it. "Hey, I've got to call Spy back!"

He nearly ran into Myrna on his way out into the hall. She saw the excited expression on his face.

As Ronny reached for the phone, he noticed Jan still out back playing with the litmus paper. It was beyond him what she could have been doing with it for so long.

Spy's phone was busy. *He's probably calling everyone about this*, he thought. Disappointed, he hung up the phone and walked back to talk with his parents. He walked down the hall and stood silently outside their doorway for a moment. Rather than speak to his parents again, he decided to go to his room for a while before calling Spy's place again. Clara and Myrna stopped him before he could leave.

"Hey, Spy said you saw a ghost," Myrna prompted. Clara interjected, "Come in and tell us about it. Don't keep this bottled up inside."

Ronny felt a little betrayed by the way that Spy was blabbing around to everyone. He thought, *Even blabbing to my kid sister. What a dweeb. If he weren't my friend, I'd pound him.* He toyed with the idea of talking to them about Beverly's ghost. Instead, he said, "Yeah. It's something like that. But I don't want to talk about it right now."

They let it drop, so he went back to his room to check the notes he'd made after his dream. There it was. He'd written that the ghost had a limp, but then she seemed able to stop it. It was as though the limp was simply a habit. He felt goose flesh crawl up his arm when he remembered what she'd wanted him to do for her. Find out if her murderer was her son or not.

He plopped down on the bed and stared out the window. Jan

came running through his door, holding the litmus paper in her hand. She was angry for some reason.

"Ronny, look." She held the paper out for him to see. "What happened to my handprint?"

He took the paper from her and examined it. Immediately he knew what was bothering her. He explained it to her. "You can't leave it in the sun for so long, or your print will disappear."

Her little face registered deep disappointment, and her lower lip started to tremble. If he didn't do something right away, she'd start to cry.

He said, "Hey, don't cry. I'll give you another piece. Just put your hand on it under the sun for a little bit, and then come back inside. Don't look at it while you're still outside. Here, come on, I'll show you."

She cheered up immediately and agreed. As she ran out of the room, the telephone rang. Ronny hurried to answer it. Jan beat him to the phone but stood there grinning and waited for him to pick it up. He smiled back and then answered the phone. It was Spy. Ronny barely got a greeting out of his mouth before Spy's excitement drowned him out.

"Everyone knows about the murder now, Normal!" Spy exclaimed. "I tried to get everyone interested in the ghost you said you saw, but everyone thought you were pulling my leg. You *do* that, you know."

Ronny didn't say anything. He did nod his head. Spy continued without an answer.

"When I told them about the murder and everything they all agreed that we have to meet at the park today. This could be big! Maybe the biggest thing ever."

Spy rushed on before Ronny could speak. "Hey, get this! You know that Rock's been hanging out with Larry Powers. Right? Well, Larry's father is a cop. Remember? He's got cop buddies in Bend and still talks to them all the time. He already knew some stuff about finding the body, but wouldn't say anything until the news broke. He told Rock that the body was found wrapped in an electric blanket, with the blanket's cord still wrapped around her neck! It looked like she had been strangled with it! The two guys that found her said that the body was gross. I mean, well, that's probably not the words they used, but, you know, decomposed and stuff. The blanket was kind of not on the body. They said that it looked like she had been beaten and clubbed. Get this, Normal! She wore a leg brace on one leg! Man, she was crippled! I hope they catch the perv that killed her!"

Ronny's goose flesh was back in full force. He remembered the limp again; the way she dismissed it by force of will.

Spy was still rattling on about the murder when Ronny realized his mind had drifted. He tried to get a word in, but Spy wasn't finished, and Ronny didn't feel like yelling into the phone to stop him.

Spy exclaimed, "The body was found on Sunday, June 15th, between 2:00 and 3:00 in the afternoon. Oh, man, Normal! Isn't that when you said you were at that cave?"

"Yes, but . . ."

Spy interrupted him. "You did say she wanted you to help her . . . right?"

"Yeah, she did say that. She spoke to me again last night."

Spy was even more excited. "Wow! Hold that for the meeting. Be there at two o'clock. OK?"

"Sure. Hey, before you go---who's going to be there?"

Click.

Spy hung up before Ronny got his reply.

It was only 8:00 A.M. on Monday. He had plenty of time to

kill. Chas should be up by now, so a visit with him was the next order of business. *No, wait a minute.* He ran into the kitchen and found his family in various stages of dress and eating cereal. David invited him to sit with them.

"Hey, Mr. Psychic mad scientist," David said. "Your corn flakes are about as soggy as a swamp."

Ronny gulped down his breakfast then finished getting dressed. He was about to leave when he remembered his promise to Jan and ran out to the garage to get more litmus paper for her. After showing her quickly how best to get a good handprint, he left the house.

He rode down the street in the same direction he and Toni had gone when they went to the park. Instead of turning right at the corner, he turned left. The Porters' house was now behind him on his right.

Chas' house was on the next street down. It was the first house on the right. As he turned right around the corner, he careened into the driveway keeping his eye out for signs that Chas might be outside somewhere.

He parked his bike on the walk next to the front door, then approached the door and gently knocked. He was in luck. Chas, short for Charles, was home. Chas opened the door almost immediately. He was of South American descent, tall, a good-looking kid, with short black hair. He was older than Ronny was by a year and already in junior high. Chas used to be the oldest member of KAUS. Spy started the club when Chas was in sixth grade. Chas liked everyone involved. He didn't care if he was the oldest. Now, however, he rarely saw any of them except Ronny.

Chas held a finger up to his lips.

"Dad's gone for the week," he pointed off to his right, "but Mom's in the study listening to classical music. You know how she hates it when my friends or I make any noises out here when she's in there." Ronny could barely hear the strains of violins from within the den Chas' parents set aside for reading and music.

Motioning Ronny into the house, he closed the door and led him through the house to the back door.

"Let's go into the backyard. You can check out my new train engine." He stopped short of opening the sliding glass door and said, "Hey, Normal, did you come over to hang out, or did you have something on your mind?"

"Both."

Chas nodded and opened the door.

His train was a Burlington Northern set. His father had built Chas a track by the side of the house under their covered patio. Ronny was partially responsible for making it look so good. Every time he came over, they inevitably spent hours working on the landscaping together. It was fun to watch the whole thing look more realistic every week.

This time Chas had a paper-mâché mountain placed in the middle of the setup complete with trees made of small sticks and moss. The goal was for both of them to take this to the Oregon State Fair and enter it for a modeling prize. Ronny wanted to enter some of his models but didn't feel ready to do that just yet.

He was impressed with the mountain.

"That looks great, Chas! Did you make it, or did your mother decide she couldn't keep her hands off, again?"

Chas laughed. "Yeah . . . Mom helped. She doesn't like making the trees and stuff." He knelt by the four-by-eight plywood board where the little miniature world was being assembled. He said, "Come on, we can work on this while you tell me what's up. I'm warning you though, Spy called me. So don't leave out any details."

Chas and Ronny worked, talked, and lost all track of time. They were both soon covered with pieces of moss, dirt, modeling glue, wood, and green paint. During this time, Ronny filled him in on everything, including Toni's involvement. Chas found this somewhat amusing. "You've had your eyes on her for a while. How come you waited so long?"

Ronny shrugged.

"I don't know . . . Shy, I guess. She's just so cute." He picked up a handful of dirt and threw it at Chas. "You should talk!" he added. "You're the one with a thing for your cousin! You're *related* to her. That's sick!"

Chas dusted himself off, then deftly flicked some moss into Ronny's face. "It's not sick . . . I like her."

"Well, she *is* a knockout," Ronny admitted. "Look, I don't care that you're weird, but your parents do. If you get grounded, worse than you are right now, they won't let me come over at all. If that happens, we'll never get this finished before the fair."

Chas raised a hand in dismissal.

"Don't worry about it. Now tell me if you've seen the ghost again."

Ronny told him about the dream he'd had last night. After that, Chas stood up and said, "I wish I could come to that meeting, but you know how it is. Speaking of wishes, I wish Dad would lighten up on the grounding thing. All I did was to peek in on her while she was sleeping."

Ronny laughed. "That's not what you told Spy. You said you were outside peeking in through the guest room window and saw her sleeping naked on top of the covers. Your father caught you peeping at her while he was walking around the yard. Man, you're lucky he lets me come over here at all. He only lets me come over because of the train thing."

Both boys were kneeling next to the modeling board. Chas stood up and loomed over Ronny. Ronny stood up and faced him.

"She's too old for you anyway, Chas, even if it was OK to fall in love with your cousin."

Chas frowned. "Well, well. Mr. Normal here thinks he can tell me that I can't have a crush on a sixteen-year-old woman?"

Ronny decided to quit this pointless discussion. He suddenly remembered something he'd nearly forgotten.

"Oh, Chas, I almost forgot another reason I came over here." He pulled the carved stick out of his pocket and asked, "This thing you gave me. You said your father told you that it has magic powers. Does it? What kind?"

Chas shook his head.

"I don't think so," he replied. "Dad was kidding around when he told me that. At least I think he was. He gave it to me and said he purchased it somewhere in Guatemala. He thought I'd like it. I gave it to you for your birthday because I thought you'd like it more than I did. I don't know what to do with it. Dad said it was OK to give it to you; that's all."

Ronny looked disappointed.

"Do you think your father was joking about the magic? Maybe it is magic. Have you thought about that?"

"Naw. Besides, I'm an atheist. I don't believe that kind of crap."

That bugged Ronny a little.

"Then, you must think Beverly's ghost is just my imagination."

Chas was a little embarrassed.

"I didn't say that." Ronny pointed at him.

"We'll find out one way or another. If I somehow prove that

I did see a ghost and then will you at least believe in ghosts?" Chas laughed.

"Don't count on it," he stated flatly. "Besides, if I start believing in ghosts, I might as well believe in God, and then I'd have to stop trying to get my cousin to---like me."

Ronny was getting a strange feeling about Chas' fixation on his cousin.

"OK, forget all that. Can I talk to your father about this stick?"

"Not right now, but I can tell you all that he says he knows. He said it was a Central American totem to ward off evil spirits or to attract and trap them. The man who sold it to him said he wasn't sure which way it worked. Either way, devils, demons, or whatever, are supposed to run away like frightened schoolgirls when they see it."

Ronny looked at it with greater respect. "Cool," he said, then tucked it back into his pocket.

"Hey, Chas, I gotta go. I'm gonna tell Toni she's invited to come to the secret meeting."

Chas cuffed him lightly on the shoulder and winked without saying a word.

Ronny smirked, "Yeah, yeah, I know." He asked, "Do you want me to go through the house or climb over the gate again. Did your dad fix the gate?"

"No, it's still busted. You still have to go through the house but be quiet."

As Ronny opened the glass door, Chas remarked, "Say hi to everyone for me . . . and kiss Toni for me too."

Ronny shook his head and rolled his eyes as he closed the door behind him.

Toni answered her door and invited Ronny inside. He had

never been to her house before, and he dreaded it now because of her father. He knew her father worked swing shift. Ronny hoped he was asleep. Not that he heard anything bad about her father. His fear was due to how Ronny felt about Toni. He was afraid that her father might look him up and down and guess that he likes his daughter — a lot.

What could her father do to him? Well, nothing really, but if he did tell Ronny to leave and never darken his doorstep again, Ronny felt he would be forever devastated. He would probably never go out on the street for fear that he would see Toni and suffer the further breaking of his heart.

Toni's father was not in bed. Ronny could smell his pipe tobacco smoke. He had to be close by and awake.

Toni saw Ronny's mind turning with worry.

"Ronny, you've got to stop fussing about my dad. He's not going to bite you." Ronny's blank stare in return for her encouragement was all she could stand.

"That's it!" she announced. "You're going to meet my dad right now! Come on."

With that, she grabbed Ronny by the hand and practically dragged him into the living room where her father sat smoking a pipe and reading the newspaper.

Mr. Daniels was a smallish man with a bald head and wore half-framed reading glasses. Ronny had seen him before mowing the lawn but had never spoken to him before now. He didn't look particularly frightening. He put the paper down as Toni walked into the room with Ronny in tow.

"Well," laughed Mr. Daniels. "You're going to throw him to the lion, I see."

"Stop it, Daddy. This is my friend, Ronny. He likes me and is afraid of you. So be nice, please."

Ronny felt pale and faint after her blunt divulgence. He braced for what was coming next. Mr. Daniels raised an eyebrow. He folded the paper and put it down, stood up and stepped slowly across the room toward the two kids. Toni just smiled and stood to one side. Ronny felt betrayed and cringed for a blow to the head, a kick in the ribs, or worse.

Mr. Daniels stopped in front of Ronny. He tilted his head down to look at him over his glasses, smiled, and then stuck out his hand. Ronny realized he wasn't going to karate chop him in the groin and that Mr. Daniels just wanted to shake his hand. He smiled back, and their hands met in a warm handshake.

"Nice to meet you, Ronny. Toni's said very little about you. She did say they call you Ronny Normal. I'm curious. Why do they call you that?"

"I guess," Ronny stammered and shrugged, "it's because they think I'm weird or something."

Mr. Daniels looked him over for an uncomfortable minute and said, "Nope, you don't look weird to me. You look like an average young man. I approve," he said, before turning around and sitting back down on the couch.

Ronny felt his old bravado return.

"I'm sorry, sir---um---what do you approve of?"

"Well," Mr. Daniels explained, "I approve of you marrying my daughter, having eight kids, and a dog and cat. In fact . . ."

"Daddy, stop it," Toni interrupted. "You're embarrassing me. I mean him. I mean---come on, Ronny. He's just teasing you because I said you were shy."

Oh, brother, Ronny thought. *When is this going to end?*

It ended when Toni grabbed his hand again and took him out of the room and out the front door. Mr. Daniels shouted after them, "Nice meeting you, Ronny. Come back at any time! Toni, make sure you close the door behind you this time, and don't stay out after dark!"

Ronny checked his watch. It was later than he expected, almost 1:30. He thought he'd only been at Chas' place for a couple of hours. Working on that landscape project was exciting and a lot of fun. No wonder he lost track of time. Toni had her bike out and ready to ride just about anywhere Ronny wanted to go. He told her about the meeting and the fact that she was invited.

"Toni, you're invited, if you want to come along. The spy club is pretty much done for anyway, so there's no point in excluding non-members from coming to a meeting. You want to go?"

She responded without hesitation. "Of course. Who's going to be there?"

"KAUS, I guess. Spy called everyone."

Without warning, Toni laughed and took off in the direction of the park. She called out over her shoulder. "Can't catch me!"

Ronny chased her without answering.

Typically, no one ever showed up on time. Besides, they were kids and subject to their parents' whims. Anyone of them could be waylaid for a chore on the way out the door.

They set their kickstands and looked around in horror. There was garbage all over the clearing, mostly beer cans and paper bags.

Toni was grossed out. "Look at this. There's garbage everywhere! Come on, Ronny. Help me get this stuff out of here before everyone shows up."

"Too late," said a voice behind them. It was Rock and Larry Powers. Rock nodded at Larry and said, "Let's help."

Between the four of them, they cleaned out the clearing and

then Rock took the machete he'd brought with him and started chopping back the blackberry vines.

Larry asked Rock if garbage was a problem every time they met here. Instead of waiting for Rock to reply, Ronny answered Larry's question.

"This didn't start until last year. A couple of guys that live near here graduated from Salem Heights last year. That is if you can call leaving grade school 'graduating.' They saw me on the trail into this park when I stopped to zip up my jacket. I passed them, so they were behind me. My zipper was stuck at the bottom, and when I started fighting with it, these two jerks yelled out that I was taking a piss in the middle of the trail. I wasn't, but that didn't matter. They just wanted a reason to pick on me. For the next few months, they followed me off and on all around the school and yelled out to everyone that I piss anywhere I want and probably on everyone's lockers. Rock put a stop to that for me."

At this point, Ronny turned and looked at Rock to catch his reaction. Rock was grinning. He remembered the events very well. Ronny continued.

"Well, Rock knew I didn't want to fight with any sixth graders, but he didn't have a problem with it at all. Besides, he was bigger than any of them, although he was my age. He waited for the right moment, crept up behind them while they were watching a girls' volleyball game. The noise everywhere must have distracted them because they didn't hear Rock. He held two small balloons filled with water and pinched closed, one in each hand.

He stood close enough to quickly unload the balloons on each of the two guys' legs. When they turned around to look at him, Rock had moved his hands in front of his pants zipper as if he'd just taken a leak on both of them and was casually zipping himself up. They were pissed off—sorry—and threatened him. Of course, Rock didn't reply. He just grinned and walked away. I mean, what were those two guys going to do? Rock could have pounded them to dust, and they knew it. After that, they left me alone because they knew Rock was my friend."

Larry was confused. "What does this have to do with all of this garbage?"

"I'm getting to that. They saw me sneak into this place when I thought no one was looking. I didn't see them watching me. They told their older brothers about what they thought I had Rock do to them and also told them about this place. From then on, their brothers brought their buddies here to party. I guess it's as good a place as any to avoid parents and police."

Rock cut in, "When we're done using this place for the last time, I say we clear out the entire area and ruin it for 'em." Ronny thought a moment as they picked up the last of the trash, then said, "That would be a good way for all of us to say goodbye to the club." Rock nodded his agreement.

They were sitting on the grass inside the clearing, talking about the good old fifth grade days when they heard several bikes, and a few animated voices, cross the park and approach the entrance to the clearing. Toni and Larry remained seated while Ronny and Rock got up to welcome the rest of the bunch. Phil, the Spy-Guy, was the first through the entrance followed by Jeremy the Brain, Louis Eyeball, Jimmy the Spit Goblin, Lorraine and Lisa, Melvin Wad, and finally Pokerface Tim.

That accounted for all of the KAUS members. The clearing was crowded, so Rock went to work on hacking a little more space for the bikes. There were plenty of blackberry bushes to go before he would be compromising their secrecy.

They were trying to get comfortable when Ronny spoke up.

"Hey, everyone. Before I say anything, Chas says hi."

Chas was missed. Ronny continued after a few lighthearted responses. "OK, let's make this quick. I know you've all heard about the ghost and what she wants. If you can believe it, I think she wants me to solve her murder."

Pokerface shook his head.

"Normal wants us to believe he's seen a ghost. I know he told Spy about the ghost before the news broke, but I still need more proof that he's not pulling our legs."

Nearly everyone muttered and nodded agreement with the notable exception of Toni and Larry. Ronny could understand Toni's lack of skepticism but not Larry's.

Ronny said, "Larry, you don't look like you think I'm crazy. Aren't you skeptical?"

Larry shook his head.

"No, I see her too." All talk ceased.

Rock stared at Larry as though he'd just farted. He said, "What? You didn't tell me this."

Larry said, "That's because I only now see her. She's standing right next to Ronny."

They all looked for what Larry said he could see, although no one could see anything at all except Ronny. Ronny turned and looked to his left and jumped a little. He was startled to see Beverly standing right next to him. She was in her middle-aged manifestation and only dimly visible, even to Ronny.

At this point, Ronny didn't give any thought to the idea that anyone else but Larry could see her. He swallowed hard and whispered, "Beverly?"

"Yes, it's me," she said, although Ronny and Larry were the only two to hear her. "I was hoping someone other than you could see me. I figured it would help your credibility, and it sounds as if at least Larry can see me. I'm going now. I can't maintain this presence very long. I'll see you later, but now I think it should be easier to get some help." Then she faded and disappeared.

Everyone spoke at once.

Larry held up a hand and yelled for them to be quiet. "Hold it," he said. "She's gone. She spoke to Ronny and then vanished. Let Ronny speak."

"Yeah," Ronny nodded. "She did say something, but not much. She just said that now I might get more help out of you guys since Larry can see her." He laughed, "Ha, Larry must be as normal as I am."

Larry replied, "Naw, I've seen stuff like that before."

Rock gave Larry a quizzical look, and remarked, "Like what? That's another thing you haven't told me about."

Larry shrugged.

Pokerface looked his usual blasé self when he objected, "I don't like it. Why does she want you, us, to help her? Why not appear to a cop or somebody like that? Why us?"

Ronny replied, "She told me that she'd tried hard to reveal herself to other people. Most people can't, or won't, see her. Maybe someone else would, in time, but she doesn't want her killer to get away. She's afraid he will kill again. So, I'm it. Unless I refuse, and I'm not going to do that. Either you're in, or you're out. Let's see some hands. Who wants to help Beverly solve her murder? Raise your hands."

Not surprisingly, there were four of the kids that wouldn't go for it. Pokerface, Wad, Goblin, and Lisa kept their hands down.

Lisa apologized to Lorraine but was patently terrified of ghosts. She left while watching over her shoulder for any spirits that might follow her. As for the other three, they waved and rode away. They didn't have much else to say about it. The spy club was finished. They all felt it.

Rock, Larry, Ronny, Eyeball, Brain, Spy, Toni, and Lorraine were all that remained.

Lorraine took this opportunity to make an announcement.

"Hey, guys! I've decided on my nickname. I want to be called Slugger."

There were moans of disapproval all around. Spy was the only one bold enough to say anything.

"That's too hard to say. We might as well call you Slugfest or Slug Maniac. They're just as easy to say as Slugger."

Lorraine was defiant and insistent.

"Well, it's no more difficult to say than Normal or Pokerface or Spit-Goblin. Besides, I'm not arguing about it. That's it." She put her fists on her hips. "Call me Slugger Lorraine."

Brain shook his head in disgust. He stared at his feet and muttered, "Girls. Geez, Loueez."

As if to change the subject, they heard a sound outside of the clearing. It was inevitable that eventually, someone other than a club member would poke their head into their secrecy during a meeting. Eyeball quietly stepped into the path and caught the intruder before he could run away. He pulled him into the clearing for all to see. It was Theodore Hawks. He was spying on them.

Apart from Eyeball, Lorraine was the first to react.

"Spying as usual, huh? Where are the rest of your spy creeps, Teddy?"

Hawks pushed Eyeball's hands away and straightened his sweatshirt. He pointed at Lorraine.

"Don't call me *Teddy*, Lorraine!" He glanced around at everyone else. "There isn't any more KRSPY. I graduated.

Remember? You can't tell me your club is still together. I just saw three of them and Little Lisa leaving just now. They looked upset."

Brain walked up to him and said, "Yeah, but they weren't upset. They were scared." Before Hawks could respond, he added, "As for the club, some of us don't need a club to be friends. I guess your group wasn't friends, after all."

Hawks regarded Brain through squinted eyes.

"How would you know?" he said and then added, "Hey, I didn't come here for the third degree."

Spy spoke up.

"Well, then, why were you spying on us?"

Hawks explained, "I was curious. I was at Larry's place when Rock called him. I know about the ghost and everything. Larry told me about it."

All eyes turned accusingly toward Larry, including Rock's. Larry jumped to his defense.

"So what difference does it make? Come on, guys! Hawks doesn't have any real friends. Why does it hurt to tell him about it? It's all over the news."

Hawks walked over and shoved Larry.

"You ass, why did you say I don't have any friends?" Pushing Larry was a bad idea, but no one expected it. By the time anyone moved to grab Hawks, he'd already backed away from Larry.

Larry was indignant. He brushed his shirt and replied, "Because it's true, that's why." He paused and then said, "Why don't you tell them why you're here, Hawks? Get it over with. Go ahead and tell them now."

Theodore Hawks looked around at the surrounding silent, frowning, accusing faces. His angry expression softened. He looked down at his feet.

"Because I want to come along. That's why."

The response from everyone else in the clearing, with the one exception of Larry, was predictable. A chorus of "Over my dead body," "You've got to be kidding," "Fat chance," "If he's coming, I'm watching my back," "I'd rather take my kid sister," and someone said, "Yeah, why not? Maybe the murderer will kill him."

Rock whistled between his teeth to get everyone's attention and then turned to address Hawks.

"If we take you with us, what will you do for us?"

Hawks grinned. "My father is a cop, remember? I told him about all of this, and he's interested. He's also a Scout Master. He even knew the Explorer Scouts that were in the area when the body was found."

Brain shook his head. "So what?"

"So," Hawks explained, "he also has a Volkswagen minivan that could take most of us to Bend, that's what. Larry's father would probably take the rest. He's also a cop and good friends with my dad."

Ronny asked, "Hey, come on, guys. Why would any adults want to help us kids go to Bend to solve a murder?"

Larry smiled and replied, "Because they think we're just a bunch of weird kids that want a trip. You know, to goof around. Hawks and I told our fathers that we all wanted to take a weekend trip to bury the hatchet with you guys and have some kicks. They went for it. Besides, it could be true. Why not?"

Everyone but Hawks looked at each other and shuffled their feet. Burying the hatchet with Theodore Hawks wasn't an experience anyone thought would come along---ever. Finally, Spy proposed a show of hands in favor of Hawks joining them.

Reluctantly, and amazingly, there were no holdouts. With that settled, they all decided to sit in a circle and discuss what they were going to do, and when.

They decided to gather at Eyeball's place next Saturday. All of them had to get permission from their parents first, but none of them thought that would be a problem. Supervised camping trips were cool with most parents. Hawks and Larry would be able to bring along four large tents and a lot of camping gear if their fathers went for it. They all hoped they would be able to find a campsite near the Wind Cave.

Killer Instinct

Waves of summer heat rippled over the vanishing point where the two lanes of a hot Eastern Oregon highway met at the skyline. Sagebrush and juniper trees dotted the landscape as far as could be seen, and a dirty white pickup truck rumbled over a shimmering rise in the road.

Luke Burma squinted through his thin dark glasses at the road ahead as sunrays stabbed through his cracked and dusty windshield. The side windows were rolled down although the passage of air did little to cool the cab or the driver. Luke wiped sweat and long stringy black hair from off his reddened forehead and neck with a blue handkerchief and then tucked it above the visor. He cursed to himself over the busted air-conditioning and the cost of a good mechanic these days.

The heat seemed to worsen the pungent odors around him. Underneath the smell of gas fumes, his black tank top tee-shirt was soaked with sour sweat down his hairy chest and beer belly. A two-day growth of black facial hair retained the odor of cheeseburgers and cola.

Burma's entire life took a turn to the road a year before when his wife of eight years left him for another man. Their marital problems began when Lois, his now ex-wife decided that she wanted to push him around. She scolded him every chance she could for not being the man she'd hoped he'd turn out to be. That was five years into their marriage. He suspected an extramarital affair and accused her of it, but couldn't prove it because he lacked hard evidence. She laughed at him for being weak and paranoid. Since that time, he found himself cultivating a rage that eventually drove him to slap her during one of her many bitching tirades. Luke was a quiet man and usually kept to himself. This sudden change shocked her, although the animal fury in his eyes stunned her even more.

As part of finalizing their divorce, they broke from the Catholic Church. Lois immediately hooked up with a man that Luke knew little about but suspected her of knowing for some time. The only thing he knew for sure was that this guy had money and plenty of it.

After that, Luke fell into a deep depression that prevented him from holding a job. He sold almost everything he owned, gave most everything else away, and then stowed what little he had left into the back of his crew truck. Now, he carried all of his possessions directly behind his driver's seat. This included a few essential and non-essential items and his most prized possessions---his carpentry tools. He believed he could survive just fine traveling from town to town between small to large carpentry jobs.

His truck had two bucket seats rather than one single. He made this alteration himself a few years back when he could afford things like that. Now he was glad he did it for two reasons. One, he liked to keep an eye on his stuff. Two, he had a rifle tucked behind the driver's seat that he could make a more easy grab for if he needed too. He was forced to pull it out a time or two, and during those occasions, if he would have needed to reach over one single full seat, he would have been dead. Life on the road can certainly kill you.

Luke no longer cultivated friends, and he remained the quiet type, with a persistent distance in his eyes. He did love music though and warmed when he heard anything by the king, Elvis. Today, he was listening to an Elvis marathon on K-GIRL, KGRL, out of Bend, Oregon.

Not only was the sun hot, but it also seemed excessively bright, even through his sunglasses. He had to squint. Filmy clouds were attempting to form, but for now, he'd have to put up with the glare that reflected off the hood and then straight into his face. He blinked away a brief illusion of someone standing in the road in front of him. Cursing, he slammed on the breaks. It was no illusion. There was some jackass standing right in the middle of the asphalt.

"You gotta be kidding me," Luke growled, opened his door, and jumped out to confront the idiot. He left the truck running.

"Hey, numbnuts! Do you want to get yourself killed? Get off my road, or I'll run you down like a jackrabbit!"

The man in front of him registered no emotion when he replied, "Your road, huh?"

"Yeah, my road! Now get off of it---pronto!"

Still unconcerned, the man replied in an even tone, "How about a lift? My rides broke down. I left it hidden off the road a ways back."

Luke was utterly stunned by this guy's inability to grasp the situation.

"What the . . . No! I'm not giving you a ride . . ."

Then he paused, shook his head, thought about it a moment, and mumbled to himself, "Maybe he's a moron or just plain sunstroke stupid."

Luke studied him for an uncomfortable moment and then spoke reluctantly. "Yeah, all right. What the hell. Get in."

He waved the man over to the passenger side door, and said, "Here, I'll have to open it for you. It's jammed."

Luke grabbed the door handle of the passenger-side rear door and pulled while kicking the doorframe up by the lock. Three tries awarded him with results, and the door opened. He stood aside as the man threw his small backpack and oddly shaped bedroll behind the passenger seat. Luke shut the door as the man climbed into the front passenger seat. He walked around and settled behind the wheel.

Luke turned for one last look at his passenger before pulling out onto the road. There was something detached about this guy, as though he wasn't there at all. He barely paid Luke any notice, although he did quietly thank Luke for the lift. His blond hair was short and neat. The face was clean-shaven though rough with acne scars. His eyes, well, they were a strange amber color. He was as tall as Luke, about 6 feet or so, although more sturdily built. He wore brown work boots, worn jeans, and a faded black denim shirt untucked and unbuttoned with the sleeves rolled up. He was deeply tanned, and about the time Luke noticed that detail, he also wondered why the guy wore no sunglasses on a day like today, so he mentioned it.

"You'll want your sunglasses. I've got a nasty glare off the hood of this thing."

Luke reached behind the seat to grab the man's pack for him, in case he had dark glasses in one of its pockets. The man reacted immediately. He grabbed Luke's arm.

"Don't touch that . . ." He smiled grimly and added, "Please."

Luke scowled but said nothing. He waited as a small red sports car honked and passed on the left, then pulled onto the road and accelerated. He glanced at his rearview mirror and noticed telltale bursts of blue smoke from the tail end of his truck, revealing carburetor problems. The corner of Luke's mouth twitched in aggravation. One more thing to go wrong with what he told his ex was his pride and joy. He remembered a conversation he had with her several years ago. Yes, sir, Lois. This truck is one of the finest made in these here United States. That was then. Now, he thought, what a pile of junk.

After a few minutes on the road, Luke turned to his strange passenger and said, "You're not too friendly, are you?"

The man stared back at him for an uncomfortable moment, then returned his eyes to the road and replied, "Neither are you."

Luke responded with a wry chuckle and asked, "You gonna tell me where you're going? I suppose you want off in La Pine to call a tow truck?"

There was a long uncomfortable pause before a reply.

"No. I'll get it later, and I'll fix it myself. It's off the road far enough that no one will bother it."

Luke shrugged.

"All right, fine. We'll leave it at that if that's the way you want it." He thought a moment then added, "You're gonna have to tell me your name, so I know what to call you, and where you want to be let off."

His passenger turned and regarded Luke with a cold expression that gave Luke the creeps. He said, "Name's Vivian, Vivian Robert McManus . . . If you must know that information will cost you."

Luke was agitated by the man's controlled menace.

"What the hell do you mean . . . it'll cost me?"

Vivian ignored him and continued. "How far are you going?"

Luke rubbed sweat out of his eyes. He said, "Arnold Cave system. Gotta run some routine maintenance on a fence and a ladder. I do contract carpentry for the BLM . . . Bureau of Land Management."

Vivian tightened his lips, sneered, and replied, "I know what the BLM is. I'm not an idiot."

That was it as far as Luke was concerned. He'd take no more of this bad attitude out of a stranger, especially when he was doing him a favor. He pulled the truck over and told Vivian to get out.

"That's it, my friend. Your crappy mouth just earned you a long walk. Get out, and don't forget your precious shit behind the seat."

Again, Luke reached back to grab Vivian's stuff. However, this time, Vivian failed to respond. He pointed at the road in front of them and said, "Sorry you feel that way. I won't be any more trouble. I'm headed that way myself. Just let me off when you turn off 18 onto 200. I assume that's where you're going. You're detouring off 97 on your way to Bend. Am I right?"

This man's audacity dumbfounded Luke. He announced, "Man, I ain't never met a man I trusted less than I trust you. I don't like you at all. I'll give you this lift, but I swear to God, you'd better like Elvis, or you're out on your ass!"

He turned up the radio. Dirt spun away from his wheels as he pulled back out onto the road. He barely avoided hitting a rattlesnake basking in the sun. Within a few minutes, the rattler was alone in the sweltering heat, and the desert was nearly quiet after the sounds from Luke's truck faded into the distance.

Within thirty minutes, they were in sight of La Pine. They stopped for coffee and a bite to eat at a truck stop, without as much as a word to each other. After a while, Luke surmised that Vivian was just one of those slow fellows that didn't like to talk. He guessed that was all right by him. Besides, he wasn't sure he wanted to know much of anything about this guy. He updated his previous feeling that the guy was weird. He thought It's best to ignore him and listen to the king sing songs from his hit movie Blue Hawaii.

Vivian didn't seem to mind the music, although there was no way to tell if Vivian liked it or not. Luke could read absolutely nothing from the guy's deadpan expression. On the other hand, his gut instinct told him that Vivian was a dangerous man.

Ten miles out of La Pine, everything changed. Vivian started to talk. It came in a rush, beginning with Vivian inspecting Luke's ashtray.

"Luke Burma, isn't it?"

Luke was stunned. He could not recall ever telling Vivian his name.

"How'd you figure that out?"

Vivian smiled at Luke's surprise. He replied, "It's on your key chain." He reached over and flicked the silver nametag with his left index finger.

Luke nodded and said, "I hope this doesn't spark you none, but why do you go by a woman's name?"

Vivian ignored him as he pulled open the ashtray with the same finger he'd used to flick the nametag. He quietly remarked, "Tray's empty, but it smells like old smoke in here. When did you give it up?"

Luke breathed slowly in and out before answering.

"Vivian, if that's your real name, you're not gonna answer any of my questions, are ya?"

Vivian replied, "I told you my name, so I did answer a question whether you believe my answer or not. Now, what about the empty ashtray? It's a simple enough question. Did you smoke? I'm just curious, is all."

Luke shook his head and said, "No. My ex-wife smoked, and so did a lady friend a month ago. I cleaned the smell out of here as much as I could."

"Ex-wife, huh? Got any kids?"

"Naw. Why?"

Vivian shook his head and raised a hand in dismissal, as though to say an answer wasn't necessary.

Silence passed for a few uncomfortable moments and then out of nowhere, Vivian said, "My mother didn't name me, my Aunt Grace did. Mom was weak. She let Grace run roughshod all over her. Grace said the name would toughen me up. I guess she would have liked that Johnny Cash song that came out this year. That one about a boy named Sue." He sneered and added, "Devil take old Grace."

Vivian paused and frowned as though the mention of the Cash song sparked unpleasant memories. When he continued, it was with an edge in his voice that hadn't been there before. He glanced at Luke and then back at the road.

"My father was killed by a drunk just before I was born," Vivian said. "He was crossing the street when it happened. Aunt Grace moved in with Mom and decided to become some surrogate father to me." He smiled at that thought. "Can you believe that? But she wasn't anything but cruel to me. I hated her, but at least she wasn't weak."

Luke wasn't sure whether to laugh or cry at what he was hearing. Instead, he opted for a forced chuckle and then said, "Man, you surprise me. Up till now, you ain't said spit about yourself. Now---well---never mind. Go on. It reminds me a little of when I was a kid."

That seemed to brighten Vivian's mood.

"Yeah? Really? What part?"

"I guess, Grace, sounds like my dad. My old pop used to come home late, drunk, wake all three of us kids and line us up on a sofa. He'd tell us to stay there while he got Mom down from the bedroom to watch while he pointed a gun at each of our heads. He always carried that gun around with him. It was always the same. He'd start with my older sister and me, and then my kid brother. He ordered us to decide which one of us was going to die. He always said the same thing, 'Don't want no more'n two kids, cause I can't damn well afford to support all of you little bastards anymore!'"

Luke glanced over at Vivian and said, "That's all."

"No, it's NOT all," Vivian objected. He seemed upset for some reason. He pressed Luke for more. "What happened? Where's your family now?"

"One day, Dad shot little Tim because we couldn't decide for him which one of us to kill. Mom and Virginia screamed and ran out into the street, still screaming. The long and short of it was that Dad ran out and saw a crowd of neighbors gathering. He tried to get into the car to run, but he forgot the thing was broken down."

At this, Luke thought of his recent bad luck with his truck and grimaced. A moment later, he continued.

"The cops chased him down. He only did five years because of some technicality. After five years inside, he managed to get another trial. The cops screwed up on the arrest or something like that, so they had to let him go."

Vivian leaned closer to Luke.

"Luke, you still didn't answer my question. Where are they now?"

Luke temporarily forgot Vivian's own reluctance to reveal his secrets. He said, "Mom died of alcohol poisoning. Virginia is some secretary out east, I guess. As for dad . . ."

Luke let his words trail, but Vivian pursued it.

"Let me guess," he pressed. "You killed him, didn't you, and no one knew about it but you. Am I right?"

Luke briefly glanced at him but didn't answer. Vivian took this for a yes and clapped his hands while laughing.

"I knew it! Ha! You're a cold-blooded killer with a killer's instincts, aren't you, Luke Burma?"

Luke objected strongly.

"No! I mean, he had it comin'."

Vivian replied, "Ha! Don't they all? Hey, Luke, I'm not saying anything about it. Don't worry. I've got a few demons of my own." He smiled an evil, oily smile.

Luke asked, "What do ya mean by that? Have you killed someone?" Before Vivian could respond, he added, "Come on, it's your turn to sing. I can't very well turn you in now can I? Besides, you've been damned unfriendly up to now, and I can tell this here's a topic you like talkin' about."

Vivian stared at him and considered for a moment. Then he laughed and said, "Why not?"

Following Luke's confession, Vivian spoke nearly non-stop over the next few miles before they got to the junction at Highway 18. Luke began to feel a little scared. This was more than an uncomfortable feeling. Discordant notes of dread harped along his spine.

After Vivian's excitement over Luke's confession passed, his voice became more controlled.

"I killed a woman in Newport two years ago. She was my second kill. She looked a little like my Aunt Grace through the eyes. She fought well enough while I choked the life out of her." Vivian grinned at the memory. "I was so excited by watching Lorna's eyes go all pale and change to gray as she died that I pissed myself then and there. Can you believe that? Pissed myself right there on the beach. Nobody would know about that though because I had to drag her body into the water---- then we were both wet. Water's good for hiding a lot of things."

Luke tried to ignore the part of Vivian's story about his pissing himself. The implications of that were too disturbing even to consider right now. Instead, he backed Vivian up a little.

Luke cleared his throat and asked, "You've mentioned your

Aunt Grace a few times now. Is she, or was she . . ."

"Was," Vivian interrupted. "Was. She died of a brain tumor before I turned ten. I'll get to that."

Luke was apologetic. "Sorry," he said. "Go ahead. I'm listening."

Vivian gave Luke a curiously conspiratorial wink and then said, "Oh, I will. I will." Then he squinted back out the window and continued. "You wondered why I don't wear sunglasses. I could tell you that I broke mine, but the truth is I don't like them. I want to see everything. Everything." He paused, gauging Luke's reaction. Luke nodded without comment. Vivian asked, "How did it feel when you looked into your father's eyes as he died?"

Luke answered without hesitation. "Good, really good. It felt like damned spring rain."

"How did you kill him?"

On reflex, Luke held up one of his hands and replied, "With my bare hands. How else? I wanted him to know that I, me, his other son, the one that got away, was killin' him."

Vivian responded, "I don't like to use my hands. They're strong enough to do the job, but they're not the first-class killing tools I like." He thought for a moment and then added, "That reminds me of my first kill, back in '63. A bitch named Judy Reever, if I remember correctly. She said she liked my California good looks. That one was nothing but a teenage slut though. I tried to show her a good time, but she wouldn't put out. She probably wanted money or something. Women. Do you know what I mean? I clubbed her a good one, for sure. A couple of times and drug her down to the river. I hid her under the bridge. The bitch had it coming."

He reached into his shirt pocket and pulled out a woman's necklace. "See this here? I took this off her. You probably think

I'm crazy to have carried it around with me for six years like this. That's six years last February. I figured this piece would give me something to remind me not to mess around with fickle little sluts anymore. Give me an older and more experienced woman. They know what a man needs."

Luke was now more than a little frightened by this man unloading all of this on him. Fears for his safety soon replaced his aggravation over how surly Vivian had been earlier. What Luke had done he felt was justified as an act of family vengeance. Vivian sounded like a cold-blooded murderer and psychotic. Luke surmised that the only thing he could do at this point was to keep things civil until he let Vivian off. The sooner, the better. Right now, self-preservation was the most critical issue. Instead of being concerned about what was irritating him, his mind shifted to becoming overly sensitive to anything that might be irritating Vivian.

"Let me turn this off," Luke offered as he reached for the radio, but Vivian held back his hand.

"No," he insisted. "Let it play; just turn it down some." Vivian stared out his side window. He spoke as if in a trance.

"I know you're wondering what Judy could have done to deserve my killin' her. Bitch tried to humiliate me. Said something about my dick." He turned to Luke and hastily added, "No, there's nothing wrong with my pecker. I didn't get my tip snipped off when I was born all. Guess she didn't like that. Too bad for her. You know, not being circumcised was Grace's idea. A right good one too. I mean, she was right. Why should a boy be cut? To look prettier? Patience, that was my mother's name, she didn't like not cutting me, but she did as Grace told her. Mom wanted to get me circumcised when I was older. She waited until I was almost ten before bringing the subject up again. Nearly TEN! Can you believe that? Man,

Grace, and Patience went at it over that one. That was the first time I ever saw Mom defend herself. Course, she had to really. Grace threw kitchen plates at her and threatened to leave the house if Mom ever disobeyed her again. Mom told her that maybe she should go, so Grace did go. She up and stormed right out of the house and stayed away for two weeks.

I couldn't believe that she left. I felt free and abandoned at the same time. The devil only knew where she went. We never found out, although Mom suspected she had something going with the sheriff."

Vivian paused again long enough to pull a red handkerchief out of his right back pocket. He wiped sweat from off his forehead and neck and then shoved it back in his pocket. While Vivian was distracted, Luke happened to catch a glimpse of something he thought was rather odd. Vivian had a length of electric cord coiled up in his left front pocket. It was poking out about an inch. He hadn't noticed it until now, because he had been deliberately avoiding anything Vivian might interpret as staring at him.

Luke tore his eyes off the wire and looked back at the road. Vivian was still talking, although Luke realized he'd missed some of it while lost in thought.

Vivian was saying, "That's funny now that I think of it. Maybe she did have some sex thing going with good-looking Ken Phelps, as Grace always called him. I guess that would explain why Grace got away with everything, all the time. I strongly suspect that was why Sheriff Phelps dismissed all accusations that Grace was the one most likely to have run old lady Shick off the road and down the cliff to her end. Well, I say, long afterlife and cheers to the late, great Grace. Devil take old Grace."

There was another uncomfortable lull in Vivian's narrative,

and then he added, "Brain cancer killed her just before my tenth birthday. I already told you that."

Luke tried to sound sympathetic.

"Sorry to hear it."

Vivian kept a straight face and replied, "I wasn't sorry to see her go. Oh, she was the strong one all right, but she tried to kill me. The night she came back after disappearing for two weeks she acted strangely peaceful as if nothing in the world was wrong. But, she had another killing on her mind. I know she was planning to kill me for revenge on Mom's lack of understanding. She was angry with Mom, even though Patience never did have me cut. Grace dearly wanted to teach her a lesson she'd never forget for arguing with her. It wasn't so much the thing about circumcision as it was about the principle of the thing. If given a chance, Aunt Grace most likely would have said, 'The point I'm making here is---which she said a lot."

Vivian waved his hands around. "Grace waited until the day before my birthday when she called me outside for a game of toss-the-ball, as she called it. She threw it out by the edge of the cliff and then ran at me as I tried to catch it before it went down over the cliff. She was going to push me right off, but Patience saw her from the kitchen window. She yelled out the window for me to watch out."

Abruptly, Vivian shouted out of his open side window, "Look out, Vivian! Look out for Grace!"

Luke cringed at Vivian's unexpected outburst. Vivian lowered his voice before continuing.

"I dodged past her as she screamed past me, nearly falling off the cliff herself. Mom ran out and grabbed my hand. Grace chased us to the car. We drove away with her screaming and clawing up the car's paint job before Mom gunned it on the main road and took off for town. About an hour later, good-looking Sheriff Phelps reluctantly hauled Grace away. The courts ended up putting her in a sanitarium where they soon found she was dying of that brain tumor. I felt bad after that. I mean, it wasn't Grace's fault. Right? The tumor might have been to blame for her being so crazy. Patience was the weak one. She should have died instead of Grace. Maybe Grace and the sheriff could have gotten hitched and made it legal."

Luke had to ask, "Where's your mom, Patience, now?" Vivian wouldn't answer him right away. There was a long pause. Something Luke was coming to expect when Vivian seemed to be seriously considering his words.

"Dead. She's dead." He regarded Luke for a moment and added, "No, I didn't kill her. Her boozing did the job." He lightly cuffed Luke on the arm. "That's just like what happened to your mom, Buddy-Luke." He laughed.

There was another uncomfortable pause as some realization surfaced in Vivian's mind. He slapped his leg, causing the already nervous Luke to jump a little.

"Hey, Luke, I just remembered. There was something else that creeped me out about that Judy slut. She didn't like where I took her! I took her into the park, and she didn't like it. Said it was too cold. Can you believe it? All chicks dig the park, with all those trees, snow in the moonlight, water, and all that crap. Am I right, or am I right?" He laughed again. "You don't have to say it, buddy-Luke. Guys have to stick together on matters of the heart. Besides, I already know I'm right."

Vivian started humming along with Elvis, which still played endlessly as if all was well with the world. Luke remained quiet, pretending to enjoy the scenery, when in fact he was trying to think of a way to get rid of this psycho, sooner than later.

After fifteen minutes of silence, it was Vivian who spoke first.

"Luke, I've got a lot more to tell you if you'll listen. I'm good at killing. How about I tell you about the last one?"

Luke wouldn't answer. He was preparing to turn off on to Highway 18. He said, "Wait a minute." He let a couple of cars pass before turning right. It was another 9.2 miles to Boyd Cave, which was his destination. He needed to get rid of this guy right now.

"Buddy-Luke, you still with me or what?"

It grieved Luke to realize that Vivian had mashed together two names "Buddy" and "Luke" as a nickname more comfortable for Vivian to say than just plain "Luke." From a guy like Vivian, a nickname wasn't kid stuff. Luke had heard about this from books he'd read. He thought The nickname is another way for him to detach me from the real world. This creep is gonna try killin' me and steal my truck. I feel it. He's unloading this stuff on "Buddy-Luke" here because he doesn't plan to let me live long enough to sing about it.

Now was the time for Luke to do something. But what? Then it came to him.

"Hey!" Luke shouted, pointing out the window. "Is that a jackrabbit out there?"

Vivian squinted in the sunlight, looking for a rabbit, but saw nothing and said so. "I don't see anything jumping around out there."

This was it — time to act. Luke stepped on the brakes and rolled off to the right side of the road. He threw open his door, stepped out, then spun around and grabbed for something hidden just behind his seat. His rifle.

Vivian looked both angry and scared.

"What the hell are you doing with that?"

"Rabbit hunting. Stay here."

Vivian stayed in the cab and watched nervously, as Luke looked both ways, then crossed the road. Vivian wasn't pursuing him. He had it good right where he was. They were heading in the proper direction, and he didn't want to screw things up.

Luke stood by the road and scanned the horizon. He hadn't seen a jackrabbit, although there were plenty of them out here. All he wanted to do was get away from that lunatic long enough to think through his next move. This guy was so far gone that he even confessed to peeing his pants over a killing. Did he do that before he killed or just during the act? That question made Luke realize just how overwhelmingly surreal all of this was. Why was he even asking himself a question like that? Luke thought, Before, after, or during---who the hell cares? He shook his head to clear it.

Luke looked around. No cars in sight, so he lifted the rifle to his shoulder and sighted across the desert. While he swiveled the view from left to right, and back again, a plan came to mind. He thought I'd remind Vivian about the blue smoke from my exhaust and then ask him if he'll help me check the carburetor while I work the gas pedal. After Vivian gets out of the truck, I'll gun it, take off, and leave him there. I'll go off the road after I get down the highway a piece, circle back and head for Bend. I'll turn the son-of-a-bitch in at the sheriff's station.

With his plan in mind, He felt ready to confront Vivian. Vivian was yelling at him to give it up and come back to the truck.

"Hey, Buddy-Luke! If you don't see any, there aren't any. Come on, man, let's go!"

To Luke's aggravation, Vivian honked the horn for emphasis. Luke yelled over his shoulder, "OK, all right, I'm coming!" He lowered the rifle and stepped back over to the truck, but before he opened the door, he leaned on the window frame and peered in. What he meant to do was to start in with his plan. Instead, his voice caught in his throat. Vivian was holding Luke's toolbox in his lap, and it was open. He'd pulled it out from behind the seat while Luke was otherwise occupied. Vivian was fingering Luke's large, all-purpose hammer.

Luke stammered. "Huh . . . Hey, what are you doing with my tools? I didn't say you could touch my stuff any more than you'd let me touch yours. Put it back."

Vivian seemed to ignore him while running his fingers over the hammer. This angered Luke. He raised his voice a little more. "I said, put that back where you found it! Now!"

In truth, the reason Luke was so unnerved by Vivian's interest in his tools was directly due to the stories Vivian had been telling him.

Vivian said, "You put that gun of yours away, and I'll put down this hammer. What do you say, Buddy-Luke?"

Luke took a step away from the door, prepared to aim the rifle right between Vivian's eyes when he reminded himself of his plan. He traded his angry expression for a forced smile, and said, "Man, you had me going there. I thought you were getting weird on me." He opened the door and climbed in a while tucking the rifle behind the seat, but within easy access, if he had to jump out of the cab quickly. He didn't shut the door all the way. Instead, he watched as Vivian shrugged and put the hammer back into the toolbox, close it, and put it back behind the seat.

Luke practically sighed aloud. Instead, he held his breath for what was next.

"Hey, Vivian, I'm getting some engine bucking. Do you mind helping me make a few quick adjustments to the carburetor before we go any further?"

Vivian considered a moment with a suspicious look on

his face. He looked at Luke through squinted eyes. What was Luke up to? If anything. Finally, he took Luke by surprise and heartily agreed to help.

"Yeah, Buddy, let's do it. But I gotta have some tools, right?"

Luke hadn't considered this. Instead, Luke hadn't even conceived of a problem like this---his tools in the hands of a psycho. Who could have imagined that his tools could terrify him like this? Vivian had him cold. Now, there was nothing he could do about it.

"Sure, grab some tools. I'll gun the engine and let you know what I need you to do."

Vivian appeared genuinely insulted by this. He objected, "I know my way around an engine. Just rev it up, and let me make adjustments on my own. I've been noticing the exhaust. Haven't felt any bucking though, but then you're the one driving. What do I know? Right?"

Anxiously, Luke watched while Vivian grabbed the toolbox and opened the door. Just before he got out, he turned and gave Luke a stern look that Luke took to mean don't try anything funny. At that moment, Luke noticed something that completely unnerved him worse than anything he'd heard from Vivian thus far. Vivian had wet himself. The front of his pants was soaked down both legs. He could smell it as well. Luke looked up quickly to see if Vivian had seen him looking at his pants. He hadn't. It didn't appear that Vivian was even aware that he'd pissed himself.

He was wrestling Luke's toolbox back out from behind the seat. Luke meant to jam the gears and take off as soon as Vivian was out of the truck, with or without his tools, but his reaction time was too slow. Cursing himself for not being fast enough, Luke watched as Vivian moved quickly to a position in front of the hood. At this point, Vivian lowered the toolbox to the ground. When he did so, Vivian finally became aware of his pants. As Luke watched in numb horror, Vivian frowned and slowly looked up at him. The expression on Luke's face told Vivian everything he needed to know. Luke knew. Luke wasn't stupid. He knew that Vivian had killing on his mind.

Luke was about to throw the truck into reverse to make a break for it when Vivian laughed and waved disarmingly at Luke while remaining in front of the truck. He was acting as if wetting himself was no big deal.

"Well, let's get this over with, Buddy-Luke. Go ahead and pop the hood."

Luke was through with being intimidated. At that moment, he decided to throw his plan away in favor of a more direct approach. He opened the door, grabbed his rifle, and stepped out onto the road. Before Vivian could say anything, Luke held the business end of his gun up and pointed it across the hood, straight at Vivian's head. Vivian stopped smiling as Luke made demands.

"All right, you crazy son-of-a-bitch. Kick my toolbox over to me and step away from the truck. Do it slowly, but do it now!"

Vivian held his hands up. "Hey, Buddy . . ."

Luke's rage boiled up his neck and enflamed his eyes. "And I ain't your buddy, damn it! Now do what I told ya!"

Vivian frowned and kicked the toolbox closer to Luke. He said, "Fine, OK, here. Take it easy. I'm almost where I want to go anyway. I'll walk the rest of the way. Just let me get my gear."

Luke considered for a long moment, then nodded and warned him, "Try anything, and I'll blow you away."

Saying nothing more, Luke followed Vivian around to the side of the truck while Vivian kicked then wrenched open the back door. He reached into the backseat to retrieve his belongings. He was partially obscured from Luke's view by the open door as he fumbled around.

There had been light traffic since leaving Highway 97. Luke was glad of that. He was more than a little nervous about being spotted holding a gun on someone. Vivian started talking again. He took his time in pulling out his pack. Too much time for Luke's taste. He began to wonder if Vivian had a gun in there. It was too late to worry about that now. He'd have to deal with it if he came up with one. Vivian pulled out the pack and dropped it to the ground. He still hadn't grabbed his bedroll.

Vivian said, "I didn't tell you about my last kill, Luke." Without waiting for Luke to reply, he quickly added. "She's up ahead at the Wind Cave. I buried her there, but that was a mistake. I want to take care of that today---take her out to the desert where I should have buried her in the first place. Guess I wasn't thinking all that clearly when I hid her. I didn't take old man Trask's advice the way that I should have. All that will be remedied soon enough."

He seemed to be fishing around in his pack. Luke was about to tell him to quit buying time, when Vivian added, "Here, just let me get my bedroll." He looked over at Luke. "The strap is loose on it. I'm going to have to fix it. Don't get nervous on that trigger."

Time seemed to pass slowly. His mind had become preoccupied from the moment Vivian mentioned a dead body at the Wind Cave.

He remembered a headline he'd seen two days ago in The Bend Bulletin newspaper. That was Monday. Sheriff Forrest Knoles had his hands full on that one.

A red pickup truck roared down the road from behind Luke. It passed them going fast enough to blow up a cloud of dust into their eyes from off the surface of the road. Luke had changed his mind about being noticed by a passing motorist. He now fervently hoped that passing truck driver had a CB radio on-board and had seen this armed standoff.

Luke snapped his mind back to the present. Not much time had passed, but Vivian was still messing around behind the passenger seat. Luke was about to tell Vivian to quit stalling, forget the bedroll and get up the road when Vivian suddenly came up with a massive hammer. He threw it straight at Luke's head. Luke ducked but managed to get off one rifle shot. The shot missed Vivian and pinged off the tail end of his truck. Vivian lunged and knocked him down, then fought to keep the business end of the rifle away from himself while at the same time straining to reach the hammer that now lay next to the right front tire. The engine idled above them as they rolled in front of the truck. Exhaust fumes clogged their labored breathing. Gravel ground into their tumbling bodies and hot asphalt burned their exposed skin.

An eight-inch lizard scuttled away from Vivian's hand as Vivian grabbed what Luke could now see was a framing hammer. In the instant that Vivian took to raise the hammer for a strike at Luke's head, Luke pulled the trigger on the rifle. He hoped to startle Vivian if nothing else. He could hear the shot ring off the left side of his front bumper and impact on the road near the tire. It worked. Vivian was distracted long enough for Luke to turn his head away from the blow. The hammer cracked pavement mere inches from his left ear. Luke rolled over, pulling Vivian with him, nearly into the street.

Another vehicle could be heard approaching from the direction of Highway 97. Luke couldn't help wondering why there was so much traffic all of a sudden.

The two men continued to roll dangerously near the traffic

section of the road. Vivian came up on top of Luke after swinging his hammer and connected a couple of times with Luke's body. An adrenaline rush kept Luke from giving attention to the pain from the blows.

A green station wagon screamed past honking its horn but didn't stop. It passed so close that both men felt its wind and smelled its exhaust. Luke tossed away his rifle. He aimed a roundhouse blow with his fist at Vivian's head and hit him hard enough to distract him. He managed to wrestle the hammer away from Vivian and tossed it somewhere over toward his rifle. Luke gripped Vivian by the throat with both hands, but Vivian had one more weapon. Vivian pulled the electric wire out of his pants pocket and fought to grasp it with both hands in the fleeting moment before Vivian brought the wire down on Luke's windpipe.

Before Vivian could bring all his forces down on Luke's throat, Luke suddenly remembered the newspaper article he read about that Beverly Winston woman. He blurted out, "They found that woman's body at the Wind Cave! The cops took it! You won't find it. It's not there anymore!"

The stunned look in Vivian's bulging red eyes was followed a moment later by a grunt of agony as Luke brought one of his knees sharply up solidly into Vivian's groin. The blow knocked Vivian away from Luke. Vivian doubled over and stumbled into the street. He wobbled unsteadily to his feet while holding his crotch and groaning. His watering eyes locked on the rifle as Luke stood up. In the second it took for Vivian to lunge for the weapon, Luke heard another sound off to their left. He turned his head in that direction just as another truck tried to swerve away from hitting Vivian.

Too late. It hit Vivian dead in the middle of his chest as he turned to face the truck.

Vivian sailed over ten feet through the air and landed in the middle of the road.

Supernatural

Vivian Robert McManus flew into the air and felt as though he'd landed on his feet. He counted himself among the strong ones to have survived such an impact without feeling a thing. In his mind, this indicated that he'd somehow joined the ranks of those survivors that wandered the Earth unscathed by the mundane world around them and therefore entirely free to do as they wished. That also meant to whomsoever they wanted. And they never get caught. He felt invincible!

The first thing he wanted to do was to get the hell out of there. No sense in waiting around for complications. He had better things to do.

For the first time since he was hit, he scanned the area to establish his bearings. He noted two disturbing facts right away. First, no one seemed to be paying the slightest attention to him, although he was standing right next to the truck that hit him. The second thing of note was that the two occupants of the truck, a senior man and woman, were bending over a body lying in the road in front of their vehicle, and it wasn't Luke. Luke was standing there right next to them, hunched over with his hands pressed against one of the spots on his body where Vivian had clubbed him a good one. So, who was the body?

Vivian moved closer and looked over the old woman's shoulder. He saw a broken and bleeding face. It was his face. He was dead!

"Good, God!" he shouted, but still, no one paid him the slightest attention. "That can't be me! I'm over here."

Vivian wasn't an ignorant man. He figured it out quickly and then smiled. Smiling. He thought about the idea of smiling and wondered if that was even possible when you were dead. Did he still have a mouth?

He turned his attention away from his discarded body and went back over to his bedroll. There it was. The hammer was out on the road somewhere, but the ballerina music box was lying on top of the bedroll, untouched. Without thinking, he reached out and grabbed it. To his amazement, it moved under his touch---and indeed, he had a 'touch.' He held up what appeared to be five stiff fingers on his right hand. Appraising himself as much as possible, he found that he did have a body---sort of---although it was naked, pale, and appeared sexless, which was okay with him.

He reached for the music box again and lifted it. He walked a distance from both Luke's and the old couple's vehicles and dropped the box behind some sagebrush. From this vantage view, he watched and listened. The old man walked away from Vivian's body to his truck. The woman stood holding her hands to her mouth, tears streaming down her face, and then stepped shakily back to the truck and climbed in next to her husband. She didn't seem to want anything more to do with this situation. She closed the passenger door behind her. Luke hobbled over to his truck and shakily sat down on the driver's seat with his door open.

After the old man finished calling the cops on his CB radio, he asked Luke if he'd mind telling them what happened.

Luke replied, "Rather wait until the sheriff gets here, so I don't have to repeat myself."

The old man nodded and said, "I'm stayin' parked right here. I don't care if I am blocking traffic." Luke nodded in agreement, and then they all settled back into their seats to wait.

A few vehicles honked as they passed. Vivian didn't want to

hang around any longer. He also decided to grab his hammer, since it worked on the music box. He wanted the necklace out of his shirt pocket but decided it was too risky. If he tried to lift it out of the pocket, one of the living might see it floating through the air. He didn't know if this would be the case, but he wasn't about to chance trying it out and being seen. Why? He didn't want the unnecessary attention right now. Vivian had no way of knowing whether or not unwanted attention could or would not cause complications. Plenty of time to find out about that stuff later.

Moving forward, he bent to pick up the hammer. Amazingly, he was able to lift it. He did this quickly and placed it behind the sagebrush along with the music box. Vivian was a little concerned that one of the living might have noticed the hammer floating through the air. Glancing around for possible reactions he was relieved to see Luke staring up at the sky and the old couple resting with their heads back and their eyes closed. No one was the wiser.

Again, Vivian contemplated his unique situation. On the other hand, was it unique? How could he know? A word came to mind. "Poltergeist"—mischievous spirits that could move things around in the land of the living. Perhaps that was it. He was a poltergeist. From all indications thus far, he was his same old self, and quite possibly more powerful than in life. This was exciting. He intended to explore the possibilities. He could well imagine a killing in poltergeist form. He could practically taste the terror.

Vivian picked up the hammer and music box and then moved further away from the trucks before continuing to the Wind Cave. He wondered why he was still attracted to that place. Did he need to see Beverly's burial site again with his own eyes? That's funny, he thought — his own eyes. But then still, he did seem to have a body. So, why not eyes?

The trip to the cave was short. It took less than a few seconds if time existed at all in whatever state consciousness this was. In truth, there was no sense of time passage. He thought about where to go. The world sped by, and he arrived at the place where he parked Beverly's car the night he unloaded her body. That was a little over three months ago.

He looked around and found what he expected. The burial spot was several yards away. The cops had the entire area taped off with warning signs not to disturb the crime scene. He assumed that they also shut down the road leading to this cave, but he could not tell if that was true.

His eyes scanned the burial site. In his new form, visual acuity was exquisitely fine-tuned. He imagined it possible to see the larvae still grubbing around looking for stray leftovers. Another thing he noticed was the new colors he could perceive. This new body, if he could call it that, was amazing. He could travel at the speed of thought and had eyes like Superman. Wonderful!

He approached the dug-up grave and looked for anything overlooked by the police and FBI. As far as he could tell, everything of any importance was removed. What had he expected to find? Nothing, he guessed. Nothing. Why did he want to find anything at all? He shrugged and turned his attention to the small cave opening.

Instead of willing himself to appear instantly inside the cave, he passed through the opening slowly. He wanted to enjoy the experience to see what it was like to travel in tight, dark places in his new form. At this point, he realized that he was not consciously aware of his two possessions any longer. They were no longer in his hands. Then as abruptly as he thought of them, they rematerialized! He did indeed have special powers!

Was he carrying the hammer and box in some way that needed no actual contact? Perhaps the force of his will alone brought these objects along with him as if he absorbed them somehow.

The narrow passage barely measured wide enough for a man to crawl through comfortably. It was pitch black, and yet he could see everything all around him. Once again, the colors, even in the dark, were astounding. He could see bugs, lichen, and small plant life everywhere he turned his gaze.

Another power he had was a keen sense of smell. He enjoyed a complex aroma of earthy fragrances all around him. Every sensory mode he'd experienced in life was heightened to the extreme in this one. Perhaps, he surmised, the human body is a filter that allows only the sensory input we need. Was the form he now had more accurate to the nature of humankind than his breathing body? It sure felt that way. If there were punishments for sin then some would say he was guilty of a crime in the extreme, so, where was his sentence?

Ha! He felt fantastic. A pestering thought did nag at him somewhere deep inside. If good things felt this magnificent, then how would bad things? One deliberation spawned another. He began to wonder if he would ever see that "white light" he'd always heard about. He was sure of only one thing. He would run from it if he did see it. There was no way he would leave this world on his own volition. He liked it here and liked what he was discovering about his newfound existence.

Soon the opening in the cave became the cave itself. It was a rocky place full of lava rock and boulders. There wasn't much to see. He thought he heard voices just below the rush of wind and voices from somewhere inside the cave. He moved quickly toward them and saw three men sitting under a bright light shining down on them from above. Was this the "white light," and these the angels come to drag him off to another world? He quickly dismissed this idea because these men were transients, and the light was from a natural two-foot-wide hole in the ceiling of the cave.

Sunlight streamed in through the hole, illuminating a shaft of bright swirling dust and a few flying insects. The pervading smell of rock and earth blended with a sweet scent of desert sage that blew in from the main entrance and then out through the hole.

Vivian watched and listened.

The three were Native American men between forty-five and sixty years old. From bits of conversation Vivian could hear, they were traveling together on foot. They had taken the opportunity to sit out of the hot sun in the cave for a couple of days before continuing their mutual travels. The temporary closure of this cave was doubtless a convenience for them. Right now, they were engaged in friendly banter and a game of poker — gentleman's bet.

They had water and dried food. One of them was tearing off a piece of some jerky. They carried this food and water in their backpacks. The dried food looked spendy, so Vivian had to upgrade his opinion of them. Maybe they weren't transients after all.

He listened. From their conversation, he could piece together that they were on some sort of male bonding trip together similar to what the aborigines in Australian refer to as a "walk-about." Vivian felt warmed by the idea of such a ritual. Men are leaving their troubles behind long enough to commune with nature, the great outdoors, conversation, and a good game of poker. Not a woman in sight, and no need of one. That was probably the best part.

The eldest of the three was a man with thick gray hair. His face was lined but kindly. They all referred to him as Pappy

Wolf. He tossed a pebble into the pot, called, and lost alongside the losing hand of the man on his right named Martin Tall Tree. Martin was jovial about his loss and let out a genuine laugh.

"Telly," Martin said. "Your luck is as glorious as your skill. I am glad we are not playing for cash today."

The winner, George "Telly" Long Tooth, smiled and collected the pot into his growing mound of stones. He was a lean fellow with short brown hair and wore a perpetually sad expression, even when he smiled.

A mournful wind blew in through the mouth of the Wind Cave and then out through the hole above their heads. Today, the wind was relatively light. Occasionally, but rarely, the wind was strong enough to mess up a card game. As long as they kept their cards down to within one foot from the ground, there was little risk of a rogue blast of air whipping any of the cards up and out of the cave through the hole.

Martin pushed back his thick black hair with work toughened hands. He rubbed the stubble on his rugged face with his fingers, then gathered up the cards, shuffled the deck, and dealt. After they considered their hands a moment or two, Martin asked, "How many, Telly?"

Telly played it cool. It was nearly impossible to get a bead on his bluff, or his bravado. He replied, "Three."

Martin turned to Pappy. "Pap, what'll it be?"

Pappy let his fingers linger over his cards a moment, then replied, "Four."

Martin said, "I'll take one."

Telly glanced briefly at Martin and spoke as casual as he felt. He smiled. "Martin, you still tryin' to fill an inside straight? Maybe someday it'll happen."

Martin kept his feelings and his cards close to his chest. He replied, "Yeah, and then you'll finally get your hand, you four-flusher."

Martin asked Telly what he bid.

Telly replied, "I bid two of my finest stones. Right here," he declared.

Pappy watched as Telly slowly pushed two very average looking rocks into the pile. Pappy's old eyes glittered with some mild amusement. He smacked his lips after finishing off a bite of jerky and then stuck out his chin.

"Call, Telly," Pappy suggested.

Martin responded by asserting, "I'll raise two."

Telly spoke slowly, with that cool-as-a-cucumber face of his. He said, "Martin, you must be up to no good. OK, I'll call." Pappy briefly considered his cards then raised four.

That was it for Martin. He folded and said, "That's it, Pap. I'm out."

Telly's calm exterior cracked ever so slightly as though the stones might be a bit more valuable than just desert rocks. He squinted at Pappy and said, "Have to see it, you sneaky sombitch."

Pappy grinned from ear to ear revealing a few broken teeth. He spread his cards out for all to see. It was a full house.

"Read 'em and weep!"

Martin couldn't take his eyes off Telly's face. Telly had been taken by complete surprise by the abrupt change in Pappy's daylong run of bad luck. Now Martin grinned as Telly muttered, "Shit a boat, Pappy. I'm impressed." He dropped his hand, which held nothing, then gave Pappy a mock beady-eyed grimace and asked, "Have I been giving you lessons? I don't recall. Nah, I'd remember something like that. Yes, I would. I ain't nearly your age, old Pap, so my memory's still pretty good." He laughed, then leaned over and clapped Pappy on the shoulder.

After a few more bits of friendly banter, they all turned their cards over to Martin. While Martin gathered the cards, Pappy and Telly pulled open their packs and dug out their water supply.

Abruptly, Pappy's head snapped up and turned in the direction of the main entrance of the cave. His voice sounded clipped.

"What was that? Did you hear something scraping around out there?"

They all listened through the wind for a moment and did indeed hear a sound that resembled scuffling. Pappy continued in hushed tones.

"Supposing those cops are back. They'll probably accuse us of disturbing the evidence. Maybe one of us oughta check it out."

Martin gathered everyone's cards into one deck and then tucked it into the pocket of his Levi's jacket. He shook his head and said, "Nah. You go if you want to. I'm staying right here. I've got a bad feeling."

Pappy stood up slowly. He was stiff from sitting cross-legged. Without a word, he walked to the mouth of the cave hugging the left side of the entrance. His eyes blinked as they grew used to the bright sun. He peered cautiously out of the cave and then chuckled and laughed. A jackrabbit was making the sounds, foraging for whatever caught its interest.

If he hadn't been paranoid of cops, he'd have recognized the sound of a jackrabbit before coming out here. Then he heard another noise; an automobile.

Pappy walked outside far enough to see the approach of a police vehicle. He hurried back inside to tell the others, and then stopped dead in his tracks.

There, just inside the mouth of the cave, on top of a boulder he'd passed on the way out, was what looked like a small silver music box. It was ornately decorative, and on its lid, a ballerina in a pink tutu was permanently poised in a pirouette.

Pappy frowned and backed away from the box. He knew it hadn't been there before he walked out into the sunlight. Now, it was. Where had it come from? He decided not to touch it. All at once, he could feel what Martin claimed he felt. Now, Pappy had that same bad feeling inside him. If someone else was sharing the cave with the three of them, then who was in here with them?

He hurried back to where his friends sat nervously waiting for him.

"I think we've got trouble," he whispered while scanning the surrounding darkness with his aging eyes. Before his friends could say anything, he added, "There are cops outside, and someone in here with us."

The other men weren't surprised by his first statement but were shocked by his last. They stood up and added their own eyes to Pappy's search as they tried to penetrate the shadows around them.

Martin spoke softly. "Was that what we were hearing? Did you see someone in here?"

Telly asked, "Pappy, why are you looking deeper into the cave? That sound was out by the entrance."

Pappy explained, "That was a rabbit. Cops pulled up after that sound." He hesitated before adding, "Somebody in this cave with us placed something on a rock just after I walked outside. I found it when I turned around. Whoever it was managed to get by you guys without you noticing, or me hearing anything behind me."

The hair was standing up on the backs of their necks and arms. Martin and Telly said they wanted to see what was on the rock, so Pappy led them to it.

The music box was gone.

Pappy held up his hands in frustration.

"It was here. I swear it. It was a little silver music box, with a tiny doll on top."

"Cops didn't take it," Martin said.

Pappy just shook his head. They all understood that if the cops had come in here, all three of them would have known about it.

Neither Telly nor Martin doubted Pappy for a second. Wordlessly, they all turned their frightened eyes back into the cave. They were now painfully aware of how the wind sounded like a moan, although they were sure that it was only their nerves. They could hear the sound of casual conversation and footsteps crunching through the gravel nearby, outside the cave. The police had returned. The three men turned their attention to these sounds, although those footsteps remained a fair distance from the mouth of the cave and did not seem to be approaching any closer.

Telly slipped away from his friends and carefully stole a glance outside the cave and around to the left. There were two sheriff's deputies outside. Telly recognized both men as Bob Lunde and Milt Neuman. All three friends within the cave knew these officers and had little to fear from them outside of the possible accusation of "disturbing the evidence." For right now though, that was enough to keep the three men quiet.

Telly returned to his friends and said, "Looks like they're pulling up the no trespassing signs. You guys want to chance to let them know we're in here?"

Pappy and Martin looked unsure.

Martin whispered, "Look, let's find out who's in here first if we can. If we say anything to Bob and Milt right now, those two will make a lot of noise and frighten whoever is in here with us. Maybe it's a kid. A scared runaway kid."

Martin and Pappy took out the small flashlights they carried and then decided to explore the cave cautiously. Up to this point, they had preserved their flashlight batteries by relying on the ambient light surrounding the main entrance and around what the locals called the "Dark Hole" in the cave ceiling.

Telly stayed by the hole while Pappy took the lead in investigating further back into the cave as far back as the other cave entrance. Martin followed, giving Pappy some considerable distance.

The only other opening into the Wind Cave was back about a twenty to thirty-minute walk, crawl, and shuffle from the Dark Hole. The body of the woman from Bend had been found just outside that smaller cave entrance.

Pappy stopped to poke the blackness with the narrow beam from his flashlight. His breathing was labored and made all the more difficult by a growing feeling of suffocation. His chest was tight from fear. It felt as though a heavy foot had stepped squarely into the middle of his chest. He hoped his heart wasn't giving out on him.

Neither Pappy nor Martin felt the need to call out to whomever they were pursuing. Why bother? Whoever it was seemed not to want to be found. It could be an animal, he thought, but then he remembered the music box.

Pappy alternately walked and crawl-shuffled over a few large rocky obstructions until he heard a soft noise in front of him. It was the sound of something being unlatched and opened. The music box, he thought. His mind developed a mental picture because he'd seen the music box with his own eyes and had an idea of what its clasp and hinges would sound like if it were opened. Pappy's hair felt as though it were standing on end. And then he heard the music box.

Tinny music violated the shadows from somewhere directly in front of him. Pappy recognized the melody as a piece from the Nutcracker Suite ballet. All three men heard it from their widely spaced locations, but Pappy was the one to find the box. His flashlight played over the rocks ahead of him until it came to rest on the box he'd seen before. Only this time it was open. The little ballerina doll was tipped back on top of the lid so he could not see it. The interior of the box was lined with purple velvet. It was empty. A sudden breath of wind blew a stray lock of his hair into his eyes. He brushed it away and reached to grab the box.

There was a popping noise directly in front of him. He froze. Something t-shaped unexpectedly appeared in the air above the box. It had metallic surfaces that reflected Pappy's light. He yanked his hand back and made a startled cry in his throat. A large hammer had materialized in the air and floated, or wavered, just above the box. Pappy yelped and tried to scramble back as fast as his body would carry him. He tried to scream, but it was difficult because of his laboring lungs. The hammer swung back as if readying itself for a blow. Then Pappy did cry. He had enough presence of mind to hang on to his flashlight, but this only managed to illuminate the horror. In a surreal moment of clarity, Pappy noted that the hammer flying at his head looked like a framing hammer. The heavy hammer cut through the air and smashed into Pappy's left temple with such force that his soft parietal bone of his temple gave way. The flat, waffled surface of the heavy hammer shattered a two-inch hole into the side of his head. Blood and brains sprayed and spattered the surrounding rocks.

Vivian enjoyed not using the pronged end of the hammer. That was too easy a kill and failed to provide that particular satisfying crunch he enjoyed. The waffle pattern stamped into the flat head of his framing hammer left a jagged tearing effect around the hole. He fought to wrench the hammer out of the old man's head. As he wrestled with it, the body looked like a flopping fish. He had to shake it loose from the skull that seemed determined to hang onto it.

Following behind Pappy, Martin managed to catch a glimpse of the unfortunate old man's bouncing body as Vivian shook the hammer loose from Pappy's skull. Martin could not see the invisible Vivian as Vivian wrestled with the hammer trying to yank it free. However, Martin could see the crushed and bloodied skull as the hammer flew out of Pappy's head, dragging bone, blood, and brain tissue with it. He could also make out a fleeting impression of Pappy's horrified eyes, frozen in his last lucid moments before a brutal death. The body dropped with a muffled thud. Martin's rocky footing would not allow him to run, but he did scream and did his best to flee as quickly as he could.

Once the hammer was free, Vivian picked up the music box, or absorbed it, as he referred to the way he carried his two earthly possessions. He moved with instantaneous speed and then caught up to Martin and passed him. Martin was close enough to the Dark Hole that the light from it acted as a backlight, silhouetting the framing hammer as it wobbled in the air in front of his face. Martin could have played his flashlight over the hammer, but he didn't want to see what that sloppy, wet gore that clung to the hammerhead.

Martin screamed again and covered his eyes with his arms. He dropped the flashlight. His screams were cut short as the hammer smashed into his forehead, knocking him out cold.

Outside the cave, the two deputies heard the screams and ran to the cave mouth with guns drawn. Telly nearly got himself shot as he ran past the two startled deputies on their way into the cave.

Deputies Neuman and Lunde allowed Telly to run by them without stopping him. The expression on Telly's face looked more like that of a victim rather than a perpetrator.

The deputies walked side by side into the cave with their guns held in front and their eyes scanning the shadowy darkness. The screams had stopped, and the only sound inside the Wind Cave was a lament of wind blowing through the Dark Hole. They stopped, felt fear, and decided to investigate the Cave's mouth before entering.

Vivian thought fast. He instantly rushed forward, up, and then out through the Dark Hole and saw Telly running away from the cave. Vivian had decided that he wanted to kill everyone today, including the cops. As he rushed forward, meaning to get in front of Telly, he inadvertently ran through him---straight through him! Amazed by this new power he'd just discovered, Vivian ran through the fleeing Telly again and again. The effect it had on Telly was a marked confusion on his face. He knew something was happening to him, but he couldn't tell what it was.

Vivian tried an experiment. He entered Telly and then stopped; and stayed in him. Suddenly, Vivian could see through Telly's eyes! He could feel a heartbeat and partially read Telly's mind. This was a possession! Vivian realized with some sense of euphoria that he now had the power to possess a living body! This was an incredible revelation. Still, he lacked any real control over Telly's mind and body. What he needed was---

Within an instant, Vivian changed his plans. He rushed out of Telly's body and raced back down through the hole. Telly would end up going back to the sheriff's station for questioning. That was not where Vivian wanted to go. Now, he had a far more exciting plan in mind, but he had to hurry.

Vivian thought he'd play a hunch. So far, the deputies had not reached the spot where Martin lay bleeding. He hadn't killed Martin, not yet anyway. However, the blow to his forehead had probably left him in a coma. He fervently hoped that all of Martin's ambulatory neural connections were still intact. The only thing Martin's body needed now was a mind to operate it. Vivian's mind.

He flowed into Martin and received an immediate reaction. Ah, my hunch was correct, he rejoiced. Martin's eyes fluttered open, and Vivian struggled to focus through a haze of pain and blood. Yes, he could feel Martin's pain. It was nice to know how much suffering he'd inflicted on the poor bastard.

Vivian/Martin managed to crawl past where Pappy lay, and then nearly back to where the other cave exit was located. He stopped, hunkered down behind a mound of dirt and rock, and then listened. The cops were approaching Pappy's body. As he listened, he heard them say that they now thought the man they had recognized as Telly, from "up La Pine way," could very well be Pappy's killer. They knew Pappy as well, and though they were confused by the possibility that Telly could have done this, they decided to follow the only solid lead they had. They left Pappy where he lay and raced out of the cave to locate and detain Telly for questioning.

Vivian was thrilled. He'd pulled off a glorious blood-red adventure, and consequently, he'd discovered more and more powers in his poltergeist form. Before he could call the day a complete success, he had to try one more thing. He attempted to absorb Martin's body, the way he could absorb the hammer and music box. He tried to will himself out of the cave while in this body, but to no avail. It wouldn't work, so he tried again, concentrating as hard as he could. No good. What he'd have to do is use the body and then leave it if he had other spectral haunts in mind. After accepting the idea that a living body reacted to his powers differently than did inanimate objects, he gave up the idea of absorption, and Vivian/Martin scrambled the rest of the way through the cave. He then crawled through the smaller opening and outside.

After Vivian/Martin climbed out into the sunlight, he lay there listening to the sounds of the sheriff's deputies driving off in hot pursuit of their only suspect. He laughed and wondered how long Martin would remain in a coma. He'd have to periodically repossess Martin, and move him around a little at least to keep him usable until his body died.

Vivian had the nagging feeling that something, or someone, was searching for him. The cops were driving away, and no one else was near the cave, so who or what was responsible for this uneasy feeling of being pursued? That feeling stopped after he'd entered Martin. One thing was sure, Vivian knew he needed to have a host body handy, whether it was Martin's body or not. He felt safer in a body. To heighten his sense of dread, while scanning the desert, he caught an unsettling glimpse of a black vortex opening and closing in the air near him. He felt it pulling on him when he was out of Martin's body, in an ethereal state.

Vivian decided that he would stay in Martin's body when he felt it was unsafe to travel in his ghostly form. That damned vortex was meant for him. He was sure of it. There was no way he would be sucked into some nameless netherworld if he could help it. This could become a real annoyance. He hoped it was a mindless portal of some kind, programmed to locate the recent deceased like an usher to another afterlife. If he fought it, then maybe it would give up and eventually leave him alone. Of course, there was the dismal possibility that there was a conscious mind behind it, or perhaps it was itself an intelligence. In that event, would it be possible for it to trick him, toy with him, and eventually ambush him?

Vivian was disgusted by that thought. Of all things, he was scaring himself! That kind of thinking would get him nowhere. He thought If only I could possess the body of a willing soul. One that could be convinced that my presence would bring him or her considerable powers, then there would be no stopping me at all! Until he could find such a person, he'd have to try to preserve the body he currently had under his control.

Foresight

For Ronny and most of his friends, the week passed uneventfully with the single exception of another ghostly visitation from Beverly. Thursday night, Beverly's younger manifestation came to Ronny in a dream. This time she was dressed not in a tutu but a shining white robe. Ronny was astonished to see her in what he thought was the traditional clothing of the deceased, or ghost. The dream environment included the secret park combined with the Salem Heights schoolyard. At this age, most of Ronny's dreams were lucid; that is, he was aware that he was dreaming and could interact with and often direct his dreams. Beverly watched as Ronny wandered around in the dreamscape, enjoying the combination of elements. Beverly was the first to speak.

"I've come to say goodbye, Ronny."

Ronny frowned. "Why? We're leaving for Bend on Saturday. Don't you want us to find your killer?"

She explained, "There's been an unexpected twist in my murder investigation, but right now I have to tell you that your parents are only going along with all of you because they believe it will merely be a fun murder mystery weekend. Theodore and Larry's fathers think it will be a kick to play along. Besides, Larry's father knows the sheriff in Bend. He's already called him and fixed things up, so, as he said, the trip should be fun. Sheriff Knoles will come out to your camp to meet all of you and answer any questions he can. I'm afraid you probably won't be able to sleuth for me this weekend. I was unrealistic. I'm sorry."

She put her hands on Ronny's shoulders and smiled.

"Ronny, they've cleared my son of the crime. He was the prime suspect, but the prosecutor failed to find enough conclusive evidence to pin the charges on him. As you might guess, I am relieved. They believe they know who did it, so I'm ready to move on."

"Are you saying you don't want us to find out for sure who killed you?"

"Yes, I am saying that. For your sakes, I don't want you to find him."

Ronny felt profoundly disappointed over her decision to leave.

"No, Beverly, don't go yet."

What he said next came without his knowing why he said it.

"I feel like something is going to happen while we're there in Bend. Don't ask me how I know, I do. Please don't go. Kids call me Ronny Normal because sometimes I know stuff, weird stuff, like right now." He pleaded with her. "Please, don't go to heaven just yet."

He and his friends were all getting in over their heads, but their parents seemed strangely blind to it. To Ronny, what Larry and Ted's fathers were doing was obvious. This was more for the parents than for them. Their parents were using what they thought of as a simple role-playing game as a means to teach them all how to get along with each other.

Beverly was beginning to fade and drift away from where Ronny stood with his back to the volleyball/tetherball court. He called out to her.

"Beverly, if you must go, would you at least answer a question for me?" She nodded agreement, so he asked, "I guess I've wondered about this when I'm awake, but I've never thought to ask you when I'm dreaming. Why do you change what you look like all the time?"

Beverly seemed happy to shift the subject away from her murder.

"I've seen many other people in this place between worlds. We are those who 'wait,' for lack of a better word. While we are here, in this place, our ethereal manifestation alters to reflect our minds. We cannot hide anything from each other. All of our secrets are made manifest to any that can see and feel our presence. Our imaginations are as equally powerful as they are unique. The intuitive subconscious is more evident here than in life. I pray you will remember all of this and use the knowledge you've gained from this experience in life."

Having said this, she vanished with a smile and a wave. Ronny felt an immediate sense of loss. What was he going to tell his friends?

Friday morning, he awoke with a start from a dream involving a man being struck and killed on the road by a pickup truck. He shook his head to clear it.

"Wow," he muttered as he shook the sleep out of his head.

"Weird dream."

He jumped out of bed and threw on his robe and slippers then made his daily trip to the kitchen for cereal. He heard his father's voice and paused before entering the dining room to listen. He was on the telephone and speaking with Toni's father.

"Yes, Mr. Daniels. I do understand how uncomfortable you must be with Toni leaving town for a couple of days without her parents. You shouldn't worry about it though; two sets of parents will properly chaperone them. Also, from what Ronny tells me Toni's friend Lorraine Larson will be coming along. I'm sure she and Toni will have fun together."

He paused while listening to Mr. Daniels and then answered one of Mr. Daniel's questions with a laugh.

"I know you think this whole spy-club solving a real murder

thing is foolish, and frankly, so do I. But I've spoken to Larry and Theodore's fathers. They're both police officers. Were you aware of that? Yes, that's right, and they plan to turn this into an educational weekend. It won't be what the kids planned on, but we both know how children are. Their imaginations run wild. I feel we can turn this into a beneficial experience for all of them. Besides, it might put an end to all that spy versus spy stuff."

Hearing that last remark made Ronny frown, and yet his father's feelings had never been a secret on the issue of the spy clubs.

There was a pause in his father's conversation, during which Mr. Hazelwood nodded and then said, "They do think they've caught the killer. Yes, that's right. Don't worry."

The conversation continued for several minutes more and involved his father giving Mr. Daniels the telephone number for Lorraine's parents. From what Ronny overheard, he guessed that all of their parents were on the phone with everyone else's parents over what they all were calling "The mystery weekend."

Great, he thought, *this trip is really for our folks more than it is for us*. Something was disheartening in that, but in light of what Beverly had told him, he felt much better about this turn of events. He wouldn't have to explain anything. He could blame *not* chasing a killer on their parents. Perfect.

His father hung up the phone, and Ronny walked boldly into the dining room.

"Morning, Dad."

"Hey, Ron. I was on the phone with quite a few of your friends' parents last weekend. It sounds like this is going to be a lot of fun for everyone."

Ronny shook his head in disgust.

"It was supposed to be serious, Dad. But that's OK. You're probably right. Besides, catching a killer is kind of stupid."

David Hazelwood shook his head. "No, not stupid. It's just not for a bunch of kids to sort out or solve. I'm sure the police will follow whatever leads they get on this case and I gather they have the killer in hand anyway. Vince and Tom, Ted and Larry's fathers, have everything well lined up and organized. It should be fun. I guess Tom Powers called the sheriff's department in Bend last Tuesday. The cave should be reopened for tourism on Wednesday. It was closed while they cleaned up the crime scene."

Ronny nodded and quietly made himself breakfast. He thought about his dream. Beverly had said that the sheriff's department already had a suspect in the case. There remained a chance that he and his friends might get in on the real inside scoop before the public at large found out. Of course, there was this nagging feeling that he and his friends still had a role to play in all of this.

His father took the day off from work to help Ronny prepare for the weekend. During the rest of the day, he received the sad news that Phil's parents wouldn't let him go along. That was *terrible* news! Philip, Spy, just *had* to come along!

When Ronny pressed the subject, he was told that Phil's grandfather died yesterday. The funeral was set for this weekend. Matter closed. Ronny knew how much Spy loved his grandfather. He felt awful for him.

The next surprise came after Ronny's father told him that Larry Powers father had a buddy in Salem, last name Tenant, that was also planning a trip to that area with his son and two of his son's friends. They might come out to their camp to visit. To Ronny's amazement, those guys were the three members of the "Cool Crew," and that, of course, meant Chuck Tenant as well. *Wow*, he thought, *this almost makes up for Spy's not coming along.*

Ronny recapped the weekend lineup in his head. *The way things are shaping up for the trip, we'll have two sets of parents along. Hawks' and Larry's folks. Then there was Hawks himself, Larry, Brain, Eyeball, Lorraine, Toni, Rock, and me.*

Supposedly, sometime during the trip, the Cool Crew and Chuck's father might show up to check out the cave. If there were still a murderer on the loose, there would be comfort in numbers.

The Bend Sheriff's Department led them to believe that all of the murder suspects were currently well in hand and that there was no reason to be concerned.

Saturday morning, two vans full of kids, four adults, and a load of supplies all headed out for Bend. They arrived at the Bend's sheriff's station just after noon. When they got out of their vehicles, they were met by bitter disappointment. One of the deputies on duty saw them arrive and stepped out of the courthouse to meet them. Mr. Hawks had not called the station since Tuesday, yet the deputy in the station that day remembered that they were coming. Deputy Norman Hatcher walked up and shook Tom Powers' hand.

"Hi, Tom. I wish you or Vince would have called before you left. We've had some changes out here since Tuesday." He smiled at everyone and waved them all inside. "Not much room in here, but you're all welcome to step out of the sun while we talk. Got some water if you all want it."

Two deputies were standing in the office area. They waved. Norman looked down at Lorraine and winked. She winked back.

Norman frowned and said, "Things are kind of crazy in here right now. Secretary's out to lunch, and it seems it takes three out of five deputies to hold down the fort when she's gone."

He chuckled, and Lorraine giggled at the idea that it took

three men to replace one woman.

They all noted the friendly but concerned expression on Officer Hatcher's face. The deputy ushered the two fathers into one of the four rooms that comprised the sheriff's station and then closed the door. The two mothers did their best to maintain some order while everyone waited for the answer to today's riddle. What changed since Tuesday?

After what felt like an hour, but was only half of that, the deputy and the two off duty officers from Salem stepped out and into a front lobby full of questions all voiced at once. Mr. Powers quieted everyone.

"Hold on, hold on. Here's what's up. They believe they have the murderer in custody, but they're not sure, so, the cave remains closed."

There were general moans, groans, and disappointment all around. Mr. Powers continued.

"That doesn't mean we can't camp near there. You know, for the spirit of the trip if nothing else. They are only concerned about the integrity of the crime scene."

After that, the mood lifted somewhat.

Mr. Hawks said, "The man in custody is the only real suspect. So, you all can relax about running into the bad guy. He's in jail already. Now let's have some fun, and let these guys do their work. All right?"

The mood wasn't as cheery as before, but it lifted again when they got back into the vans and headed to the fast food restaurant for hamburgers.

Deputy Hatcher was joined at the front desk by Deputy Jean Patterson. They watched as the two vans pulled away from the curb and drove off. Norm Hatcher was already seated in front of a pile of paperwork when Bob Lunde entered the room and sat down next to him.

Bob said, "We shouldn't have let them go out there. We still haven't found Martin. What if Martin is out there somewhere like Telly said he was? What if Martin killed Pappy? All Telly's blabbering about a ghost in the cave and a music box sounds like an overactive imagination, but, all the same, I don't like it."

Deputy Lunde reentered a common room occupied by a man named Luke Burma. Luke sat at a table, waiting for the deputy to return. He had been called back to the station to answer a few more questions.

"OK, Luke, now tell me again. Why don't you think we have the right man?"

Luke sat back in his chair and stared flatly into the deputy's eyes.

"Because I know Telly, and he couldn't do what you said was done to Pappy. I know this sounds crazy, but if Pap was murdered the way you said, well, that's how Vivian said he preferred to kill people."

Bob Lunde shook his head in disbelief. "You mean the dead guy? You want me to believe that the guy that got creamed on the road by Dean and Alice last Wednesday is the same guy that killed Pappy? Is that right? That's your bottom line, Burma?"

Luke took a deep breath and exhaled with resignation.

"No, of course not. I mean, well, I'm not sure what I mean. But . . ."

He stopped to consider his words before continuing.

"I'm just saying that I believe what Telly is telling you. I do think Martin is still out there somewhere, but I don't believe he killed Pappy either. We've got to find Martin if we want all the answers."

Deputy Lunde pulled out a chair and sat down across from Luke.

"Luke, I'm willing to believe that Martin is the real mystery at this point. That is if you're right and Telly didn't kill Pap. So we'll follow up on that and give you a call if we have any more questions. Is that OK with you?"

Luke nodded and stood up. As he left the room, he turned around to add one last question.

"Vivian's hammer, the one he nearly killed me with, have you found it yet?"

Bob regarded him a moment and frowned. This was the one mystery from the scene of the accident. He replied with some hesitation, "No. Not yet."

Luke said, "You should have seen that creep's eyes. By the way, you'd better find that old man Trask that I said Vivian was talking about. From what he said, it sounded like the old man coached Vivian before he murdered Beverly."

Luke turned away from the silent deputy and left the building. Luke's reference to old man Trask bothered the deputy and left him in a quandary. Lenny Trask and that was the only old man Trask he knew of, did have a colorful past, although, Lenny was now a devout AA convert and as trouble-free a fellow as Bob Lunde had ever met. He didn't see any reason to bother the old man. Then again, what would it hurt? Lunde decided to track Lenny down for a little chat. He should be easy enough to find down at the alcohol-free club.

Deputy Bob Lunde waved off a bad joke from Norm Hatcher as he left the building. Bob shook his head. Norm had to get a handle on his weird sense of humor. Within fifteen minutes, he was in sight of the club. He spotted Trask walking along the sidewalk on the right side of the road. Trask was tall and wore denim with brown work boots. He had an old cowboy hat pulled down in front and about a week's worth of stubble covering his face. His old gray eyes caught sight of the deputy's car.

He frowned and tried to ignore it. Deputy Lunde pulled slowly over to the curb and rolled down the passenger side window. He leaned over the passenger seat and called out for Lenny to hold up a minute.

"Hey, Lenny! Would you mind talking with me a minute? This won't take long."

Trask shook his head without slowing in his stride.

"Sorry, deputy. I've got business to tend to."

Lunde wouldn't let up. Something was disturbing about the way Trask avoided his eyes. Deputy Lunde pulled over and stopped. He quickly climbed out of his patrol car and crossed in front of it to block Trask's way. Trask tried to walk past him.

"I hate to do this to you, Mr. Trask, but I'm afraid I'm going to have to ask you to stop walking and listen to me. I don't want to detain you any more than I have to."

Trask stopped and spun around to confront the deputy.

"What is it you want, Bob? I'm late."

"For an AA meeting?" Bob asked.

Trask squinted and replied, "That's right."

"Then skip one today," the deputy insisted. His impatience was showing when he added, "Seems as if you're nervous about something. In about five seconds I'm taking you down to the station for questioning; that is unless you cooperate with me right now."

Trask hesitated and then softened slightly.

"Alright, Bob. Let's get it over with. What's the problem?"

The deputy studied Trask's face for a long moment before proceeding. "Beverly Winston's murder. A source said a guy named Vivian Robert McManus fingered you as his mentor and said that McManus confessed to killing Beverly. McManus claimed that you coached him."

Bob Lunde watched Trask's face for some sign betraying fear. If Trask was afraid of anything, he didn't show it.

Trask looked thoughtful. He glanced down at the sidewalk, across the street, and finally back at the deputy, before answering.

"Yeah, I knew McManus. He was a psychotic lunatic." Trask smiled at some private thought, and added, "He could have killed that woman for all I know, but I had nothing to do with coaching him." Trask nodded toward the club down the street and said, "Now, unless you have more than that to accuse a man with, I suggest you let me be about my business."

The hot sun beat down on the two men during their brief and silent stalemate. The deputy silently struggled with the thought of hauling Trask in on a trumped-up charge, but let it drop, for now.

"You know, Trask, I've never had cause to mistrust you as I do now. I know about your checkered past with biker gangs so that I could haul you in on a hunch." Lunde's eyes held Trask's dull stare. "If you leave town, Trask, I swear to God I'll find you, and then I'll lock you down until this is cleared up. Do you get me?" Trask nodded, but Deputy Lunde continued. "I think you do know something about this."

Trask smiled and said, "Even if I did, you can't pin anything on me. Besides, Vivian is as dead as Miss Annie's libido. You can't verify a thing."

The deputy was shocked. "How did you know about his death?" he demanded. "That wasn't made public."

Trask was casual in his reply.

"Word gets around, deputy. Yes, sir. 'Word'---it does get around some." He continued to smile when he added, "I wouldn't count on that boy Vivian's soul to rest comfortably."

Trask mumbled something, and then added,
"The boy's got too many demons."

Moonlight

The two vans carrying Ronny's enthusiastic load of friends drove Highway 18 to the Lavalands Visitor Center and then on to the Lava River Cave and Lava Butte. As indicated by the sheriff's department, the Arnold Lava Tube System was closed to preserve any evidence in the Beverly Winston and Pappy Wolf cases. Those lava tubes included both the Wind Cave and the adjacent Bat Cave. They did explore the two caves closest to the Arnold system, Boyd Cave and the Skeleton Cave. After that, they drove to Sand Springs and Lavacicle Cave. It was a full day by the time they arrived back at their pre-determined campsite at 7:30 P.M. At that time of the year, they had an hour of sunlight left in their day.

The two fathers felt comfortable with the way the murder investigation was shaping up. By all accounts, the killer had been found. They felt perfectly safe camping less than 1/8 of a mile north of the Arnold system. It was decided that Toni and Lorraine would share a large tent with Mrs. Powers and Mrs. Hawks. Ted, Larry, and Rock would all share one tent, while Ronny, Jeremy the Brain, and Louis the Eyeball would share another.

The fourth tent was set aside for Tom and Vincent. Both men remembered what it was like to be boys. An adult in the boys' tent would be accepted, but not welcomed, and certainly not that much fun for the adults either.

Larry and Rock unfolded a card table. Everyone pitched in to create a meal of beans, hot dogs, canned corn, soft drinks, and potato chips. After eating, they all settled around the campfire, on folding campstools, for what the two fathers promised would be a scary story that happened. Mr. Powers' brother Gary had been present when the events in his story occurred. Mr. Powers' brother. Gary related the story to Tom just after Gary returned home from the most frightening trip of his life.

Toni sat close to Ronny with her arm curled around his. Jeremy and Louis watched her snuggle into Ronny's shoulder with unveiled amusement while Ronny tried to act nonchalant. He was blushing nonetheless. Toni saw this, smirked, and picked up a handful of dirt which she tossed at the two gawkers before they could duck. Gloria Hawks gave the two boys a stern look intended to tell them not to throw anything back at her and gave Lorraine an equally fierce glance for throwing something in the first place.

While Tom Powers told his story, Mr. Hawks provided occasional sound effects. This included rocks tossed into the surrounding desert or different animal noises. The girls hated this, and by the middle of Tom's story, so did the guys.

Mr. Powers set the mood for the story by asking, "Why do you think places like this seem haunted?"

All eyes roamed the shadow-soaked moonlight parameters of the camp.

Toni was the first to answer.

"Well, I suppose it's because of the wind and shadows." She shivered. "The bats squeaking and flying all over the place is pretty creepy too."

Toni added, "I hear coyotes or dogs somewhere over there."

She pointed over her left shoulder.

"Come on," Jeremy objected. "The reason this place feels haunted is that we're so close to where they found two dead bodies. Geez, Mr. Powers, do we have to have a ghost story tonight at all? This whole trip feels like a ghost story, and it's freaky enough around here without another one."

Tom smiled. He replied, "This isn't a ghost story, Jeremy. It's a true story and doesn't even have a ghost in it."

Jeremy was defiant. "Yeah, what of it? It's going to be scary, so what's the difference? Geez."

Mr. Powers remained silent and turned his head searching the surrounding darkness, seemingly for effect. It worked. There was an uncomfortable lull while all necks craned to see where he was looking. They heard crunching sticks, pine needles, and rocks outside their camp. Mr. Hawks assured them all that the noises were probably small harmless animals and nothing more. Both of the mothers had slight smiles on their faces. Tom Powers could see by the kids' expressions that the time was right to begin his story.

"Let *me* tell you why places like this seem haunted." He paused for effect. "What you are feeling is not the presence of someone or something, but rather how out-of-place *you* are." He gestured to the trees around them. "This home belongs to the creatures of the desert, and you are haunting *their* world. Sure, you may not be ghosts, but to the creatures that live here, we are just as threatening." He studied their happy faces for a few seconds, and then said, "I'm going to tell you a story that took place during summer, two years ago, at another campground far from here. My brother, Gary, led a group of six Explorer Scouts into the California Sierra Mountains. He directed them off the established trails and into what the '*wilds were all about*. Trailblazing. They were looking for a small group of four cabins high above the tree line. These cabins were used several times a year by the Forestry Service but were vacant that month.

"By the time Gary and his Scout troop cleared the ridge near the cabins, all seven of them were exhausted from the long hike up the mountain. They climbed onto a jumble of large boulders to catch their breath and survey the area. Gary had promised them an uncluttered view that would be nothing short of wide-open vistas as far as their eyes could see, and they were not disappointed. The view was unparalleled by anything they had seen so far on that trip.

"It was late in the evening, yet the sun had not yet dropped below the horizon. It would do so in an hour. They spotted the group of four cabins nestled among the scrub brush approximately one hundred yards away, just as Gary had described it. They were all as excited to investigate as you were to visit the Wind Cave."

Tom pointed at Jeremy with mock anger on his face. "Don't say anything, Jeremy." He then cast a theatrical glance over his shoulder and continued the story.

"They had their campfire, the cabins, and not much else. The first job was to make sure the cabins were secure inside and out. While one of the boys made a fire, Gary organized any repairs he suspected they would have to make. He brought a few light tools, nails, and other supplies they'd need to make some minor repairs.

"Within a short time, they established what they believed to be a safe campsite. The cabins were well kept and needed only a few boards nailed back into place. The buildings were roughly 12 feet square and ten feet high, with flat roofs made of wood and green fiberglass roofing materials, which were poorly conceived considering the frequent buildup of snow. The Forest Service had plans to replace or reinforce the fiberglass.

"The doors were padlocked, but Gary came ready with keys in hand. The Forestry Service enjoyed allowing Explorer Scouts the use of these buildings because they always left the premises in better shape than they found them.

"By sunset, they settled in for a meal around the fire. There was a relatively small mountain lake for water. They ate dried meat, dehydrated vegetables, and potatoes from the supplies they all carried, and they were looking forward to fishing the next day."

Lorraine interrupted Gary's narrative with, "Gross! That stuff sounds awful!"

Gary was about to resume his narrative when Jeremy took the opportunity to complain again.

"Come on, Mr. Powers, you're telling us a scary story with a bunch of guys sitting around a campfire, to all of us, sitting around a campfire. That's a cheap shot to creep us out. Geez."

That was all Louis could stand from Jeremy. He gave Jeremy a hard shove that knocked him off his folding chair, and into the dirt. Jeremy jumped back up and dusted himself off. Mr. Hawks pulled them apart.

Louis said, "What are you, Brain, some chicken brain, or what? Why do you keep on flipping him crap? We all want to hear this story, except for you. What's your problem?"

Jeremy complained and continued to glare at Louis while muttering something about Eyeball never touching him again, or he'd poke those huge eyes right out of his head.

Tom cleared his throat.

"Now," he resumed, "while they were all sitting around the campfire, Gary, my brother, for all of you that forgot that fact through all of these interruptions, mentioned a report the Forest Service made about some trouble about a mile from where they were sitting around that very campfire. It involved one of their employees who went crazy and was hiding out in the Sierras somewhere. Every year, for about ten years, a Forest Service employee by the name of Dan Web routinely inspected a fifty-mile portion of the Sierras for summer fire hazards. That land included the very same grouping of four cabins that Gary and his scouts were just then using as their base camp. As it happened, there was a cliff that dropped straight into a ravine about one half a mile to the east of that camp. It was at least a thirty-yard fall if you were unlucky enough to lose your footing while looking over the edge.

"One day, Dan was walking near that cliff when a black bear came roaring out of the woods. It was probably a female bear protecting her cubs. Later, tracks around that location supported that theory. Dan had nowhere else to go but down. He tried to slide down the side of the cliff to escape the bear, but it was too steep. He fell hard and hit his head on an outcropping of rocks. Of course, the bear didn't follow him. By sheer luck, some hikers stumbled across him and found him barely alive. One woman stayed to dress his wounds with a first aid kit. The other two women hiked back down the mountain to their base camp, alerted the rest of their group, assembled a stretcher, and then enlisted three volunteers to help carry Dan back down with them. By the time they arrived at the spot where they had left Dan, and their friend, neither of them were anywhere to be found.

"Searching the area, they located two sets of tracks leading around the base of the cliff. They followed them to one cabin in the grouping of four. Dan had awakened with enough strength to walk and guide the two of them to the nearest shelter. Gary pointed out a cabin furthest away from where he and his scouts sat around the fire and told them that they found the woman in that cabin, strangled to death, and no trace of Dan. They did find Dan's tracks, but they ended in an area choked with debris.

"All they could deduce from available evidence was that for some unknown reason Dan turned on the woman, strangled her, and then fled. The woman's friends performed a thorough search of the cabins but failed to find any substantial clues as to what happened. They carried their companion's body back down to their camp and then into town. When they reported the incident, the sheriff's department became involved, and a search was underway.

"The chase for Dan was extensive but failed to locate him. There were scattered reports of animals that had been butchered, dressed out, and used for meat. Carcasses were occasionally found hidden in bushes and hastily concealed with dirt and rocks. Eventually, deputies found a discarded bandage covered in dried blood. These were probably Dan's head wound dressings.

"Reports continued to pile up in the sheriff's office of a wild man living and hunting in the Sierras. Dan was managing an expert job of avoiding capture. Months passed. Two more hikers were killed, and yet it was difficult to tell if they were victims of an animal attack or if Dan was responsible. These incidents were reported further and further south. Officials followed whatever trail they could and then abruptly all signs of Dan disappeared. No more kills, animal or human. It was surmised that he must have suffered a concussion and severe brain damage from the fall, and that had resulted in psychosis. He might have died somewhere from complications.

"At this point, Gary's six Explorer Scouts became visibly shaken. They wanted to know if Dan's body was ever found. Gary said that he had to admit that no trace of him had been found. Technically, Dan was still out there somewhere, dead or alive. A couple of Gary's scouts batted around the idea of mounting a search of their own for Dan's corpse. The rest of the troop quickly dismissed that.

"After that story, Gary tried to move on to lighter discussions on merit badge projects, but the story about Dan Web remained on everyone's mind. So much so that they all stopped talking about the assignments and took up the topic of Dan again. Gary told his scouts that Dan most likely used his forestry and tracking expertise to lead his pursuers off in one direction but withdrew in an opposite route. Dan was probably hundreds of miles away, or, more likely dead. With that in mind, they all relaxed a little and discussed the next day's itinerary, including who was in charge of breakfast. One half-hour later they broke down the fire and covered it with large rocks. This would keep sparks from flying out and preserve some coals for the morning. Gary decided to take one cabin for himself while the boys took the other three.

"Just as Gary opened the door to his cabin, he heard a loud cracking noise coming from one of the other cabins. Shouts of alarm told him to turn around and run back to see what was going on. Scouts emerged to join him as he ran to where all the shouting was coming from. They all converged where two Scouts were standing in the doorway of one of the cabins. They pointed in through the door. Inside, the cabin roof had caved in near the back wall. Moonlight streamed in through a hole in the ceiling. Hanging down through that hole was the arm of a skeleton, ending in the dangling skeletal remains of a hand.

"Gary shouldered past his scouts, stepped cautiously inside, and scanned the cabin by flashlight. As he drew near the hole, he felt a cold chill pass through him. Strangely, the chill seemed confined to the shaft of moonlight streaming in through the hole in the ceiling. Gary looked up and saw that a skull, retaining fragments of beard, dried skin, and long black hair, seemed ready to follow the arm down through the hole. Then Gary noticed the watch on the bony wrist. It was a Rolex. Carefully, Gary turned the watch so that he could see if there was an inscription. His suspicions were realized when he read

'*To Dan with Love, Lydia.*' The chill air that seemed to hug the shaft of moonlight grew colder. Gary left the cabin and locked it. No one slept well that night."

Tom Powers finished his story. This time Rock spoke first.

"Excuse me, Mr. Powers, but why did the roof collapse just when the boys opened the door?"

Tom shrugged.

"Well, perhaps . . ." Jeremy broke in.

"Oh, hey, everyone, I've got an explanation for you. It was spooky! What else could it be? That's also why that shaft of moonlight was so cold."

Tom stopped Jeremy by holding up a hand.

"No, Jeremy. Not spooks. Gary said he thought it was all of the hammerings on the wallboards during repairs. The roof may have been weakened. Opening the door may have been the final vibration necessary to cause a collapse."

Toni asked, "Wait a minute. Why did that guy climb up on the roof to die?"

This time someone other than Tom offered an answer.

"Maybe Dan was trying to repair the roof himself when he died," Ronny offered.

Tom nodded. "You're probably right about that, Ronny. Officials that came for the body did find loose boards, nails, and a heavy rock up there. He must have been using the rock as a hammer. Good guess."

Tom looked over at Jeremy, who had scowled through the whole story. Jeremy remained agitated over Louis pushing him off his stool. Mrs. Hawks took the opportunity to say something to lighten his mood.

"Jeremy, there weren't any ghosts in the story, and Louis pushes you all the time, so cool it and smile a little."

Jeremy hated that *let's get smiley* kind of stuff, but he refrained from being rude. Instead, he shrugged and replied, "Well, I don't know what you call that cold spot stuff. That sounded like Dan Web's ghost was lurking around in the cabin to me."

Tom interrupted him. "It was probably their nerves, Jeremy. In any case, everything turned out OK . . . so relax."

Louis wasn't going to let Jeremy get off the hook quickly.

"Hey, Brain, if spook stories freak you out so much, then why did you come on this trip? Scaredy Cat!"

That question from Louis brought a round of agreement and heads nodding from everyone, including the parents. Jeremy was on the spot. He stood up and defended himself.

"Leave me alone. I came along because I thought it would be fun. Now, I think we're in the wrong place at the wrong time. Maybe we should have gone home after talking to the deputies. I mean, come on! They don't even know if they have the right guy. Geez. For all we know, the killer could still be around here somewhere."

He lifted his hands, indicating the darkness that surrounded them. "Hasn't that occurred to any of you? Yeah, that creeps me out a lot. Besides . . ."

At this point, Jeremy pulled a small handheld electronic device out of his pocket.

". . . This thing," He continued, "is flashing red now and then. It's not supposed to do that, unless . . ."

He paused, unsure how his next statement would be taken.

"Well, I made it from drawings and schematics I found in one of those weird magazines Eyeball always buys." He looked at Louis, and added, "You know the one I mean. It's that one about ghosts, flying saucers, and creepy stuff. This thing is not supposed to light up red unless there are ghosts around." He held it out for everyone to see, and said, "OK, so it's not blinking red right now, but it was about an hour ago. So, will you guys give me a break? I'm a little on edge right now."

As if on cue, startling everyone, they all heard and saw automobile headlights approaching their campsite. It was the sheriff's car. Sheriff Frank Knoles got out of the patrol car. He was alone.

He waved and walked over to the campfire.

The sheriff greeted everyone cheerfully.

"Hi, betcha thought I wouldn't show. Sorry, I'm so late, but I figured you all are in good hands with Tom and Vince here and can't stay long. I just wanted you to know that we believe we do have the killer in hand, and you are all perfectly safe here."

Rock raised his hand, as though he was in class. He suddenly realized how silly he looked and lowered his hand. Sheriff Knoles saw him and smiled. Several of the kids laughed, but Frank Knoles put Rock at ease.

"No need to stand on formalities," he said. "You have a question?"

"Yeah." Rock collected his thoughts, frowned, and continued, "Mr. Hawks said that there might be someone else out there, someone that you can't find. A guy named Martin?"

The sheriff's brow knitted for a moment. He looked down and then back at Rock.

"No. We *don't* believe Martin is out here. We scoured the area and didn't find anything significant. Martin is not in the area. Telly and Pappy must have had a fight, which happened often enough anyway, and Telly cracked his head open with a rock. It's that simple. Anyone that knew those two could remember the many times when Telly threatened to kill Pappy over one small thing or another. We always passed his threats off as harmless because they were friends as far back as anyone can remember. We should have taken Telly's threats seriously."

Larry joined in with a question of his own.

"So, can we explore the cave? I mean, is it still against the law or something?"

Frank Knoles shook his head and said, "We got all the evidence we could get out of that cave. I don't think we have a right to keep you all from exploring what you came out here to explore."

Theodore Hawks raised a question that left everyone unnerved.

"What about Beverly Winston? We're all forgetting about her. Did Telly kill her too? Where is her killer?"

For a moment, everyone was silent. Little noises from the surrounding desert punctuated Theodore's question. The sheriff's answer sounded more than a little forced.

"Now, that's a good question, and I have a good answer. We believe the man that killed her is dead. He died after being hit by a truck not far from here. That's all I can tell you. There's no need to be concerned over that one. For a while, we thought it might have been her son that killed her, but we couldn't find any hard evidence to that effect. Now, well, we have a reliable witness that spoke to the guy that killed her. The suspect more or less confessed to it before being struck and killed."

Ronny heard this last detail and remembered his dream about a guy being run down by a truck. He knew this was important, so he tucked the memory away for later.

Louis had been drawing in the dirt with a Y-shaped stick. He shook his head, looked into the darkness surrounding the camp, and responded to what the sheriff had just said.

"No, I don't believe it's over yet. You think you caught the guy, but I think he's still out there somewhere. I can feel it."

Mrs. Powers was upset by what Louis said. She scolded him.

"Louis, you shouldn't scare everyone that way. You've just heard Sheriff Knoles said that the killer is dead. Why do you need to be so negative? Now you sound like Jeremy."

The Jeremy remark stung Louis into silence and played across his face like a betrayal. He stared at her a moment and then lifted his stick and pointed with it out over the desert.

"I think that woman's murderer is a ghost now," Louis replied, "and I think he's been watching us the whole time we've been here. I can feel it. Don't ask me how." He looked at Jeremy, with a pained expression on his face, before adding, "I hate to admit it, Brain, but you might be right."

Mrs. Powers leaned toward Louis, smiled a parent's smile, and said, "Everyone says you have a kind of special sense for some things, Louis, but I think, just this once, this whole thing has you unnerved, and you imagine things."

She reached out and touched his arm. "Don't you think that's possible, Louis?"

Despite her efforts, everyone, including the adults, appeared noticeably unnerved by what Louis and Jeremy said. Sheriff Knoles chose this moment to say goodbye."Enjoy the cave tomorrow, folks. Everything's under control."

Dust obscured his taillights as everyone watched him leave. Despite Louis's forced apology, Jeremy took this opportunity, while everyone was distracted, to get even with Louis for pushing him off *his* chair. He shoved Louis off his chair and then stood over him and said, "You're a creep, Eyeball! Why'd you have to go and scare everyone like that?" Louis jumped up and stood chest to chest with Jeremy and shoved him back.

"Me?" he yelled. "What about you?"

Jeremy balled up his fist and took a swing at Louis's head, but Louis ducked it. At this point, both fathers intervened. Tom grabbed Louis, and Vince held Jeremy.

"Knock it off! Both of you!" Vince insisted. "Or we'll tie you both up for the night."

Tom said, "Are you guys done, or do I get the rope?"

Both boys nodded reluctantly. Jeremy asked Mr. Hawks if he could sleep in one of the vans rather than having to sleep in the same tent with Louis. His request was denied.

Ronny found Louis fiddling with his Y-shaped stick on the edge of the camp, facing the direction of the Wind Cave. Ronny interrupted his thoughts.

"Hey."

Louis looked over at Ronny and then stared back into the dark landscape.

"Yeah, Normal. What's up?"

Ronny nodded at the stick. "What are you doing with that thing?"

"This?" Louis asked, with a thinly veiled smile. "Oh, it's a ghost finder. Kind of like Brain's, only about a thousand times better."

Ronny shook his head.

"What's with you two guys?" He indicated the desert with his hands. "Why all that competition now?"

Louis seemed to hurt.

"What do you mean? You know why. Brain has been trying to outdo me when it comes to my interest in weird stuff. Now he wants to say he's better at finding ghosts. He should stick to the transistor geek stuff."

"OK, you're the weirdo," Ronny said, "and he's the nerd. I got it, and so does everyone else." Ronny pulled out the South

American totem stick Chas had given to him. He pointed at it and asked, "So, what do you say about my bringing this along? Chas says it's supposed to have magic powers, but he doesn't believe in that kind of thing. Does my bringing this stick make me competition?"

Louis grinned.

"Hey, that's right! I forgot all about that thing. No, you're not competition. Brain is, or wants to be." He paused and then added, "If Brain doesn't stop wimping out, he's gonna jinx us."

"He'll be all right."

Louis didn't look convinced.

"Yeah, sure." His eyes brightened, and he held out a hand to Ronny, with his eyes on the totem. "Can I see that thing a minute, please?"

Ronny shrugged and handed it to him. When Louis held it in his hand, there was a sudden change in his facial expression. He went from fascinated one second to terrified in the next and quickly handed it back to Ronny.

"Here, take it back."

"Why, what's wrong with it?" Louis wagged his head. "It's probably nothing. But, oh, something about it feels wrong, like there's something *in* it. I don't know. Forget it."

Ronny held the stick up for a closer look. The dark wood was carved in a fashion similar to many giant stone stelae found in and around Guatemala. It looked like a stylized man with a big head, large eyes, and a flat nose, surrounded by bold design work. There was nothing overtly special about it.

"I don't feel anything strange," Ronny remarked.

Louis poked Ronny in the chest. "You might not, but I do. Just be careful of that thing."

Louis returned his attention to his y-shaped stick. He held it out in front of him with both hands. Ronny watched with interest as Louis explained that it worked just like a divining rod.

"I hold on to both ends and wait for the other end to tug in some direction or another. That's how it finds ghosts."

Rock, Larry, and Hawks helped the adults to clean up the campsite. Ronny waved at Jeremy who was wandering around and talking with Lorraine. Her hands were animated as she complained about the way everyone forgot to call her "Slugger." Ronny was glad not to be sharing the brunt of Lorraine's wrath. He turned his attention back to Louis.

"Brain's black box picked up something a while back. Did your divining rod catch anything?"

Louis replied without looking at him.

"I didn't want to say anything when he mentioned that red light, but yeah, it did. This thing pulled in the direction of the Wind Cave. That's the reason I believe this area is haunted. I can feel it, can't you?" He didn't wait for Ronny to respond before adding, "I do think there's something out there, and I think it's a ghost."

Toni walked over and interrupted.

"Hi, guys. What's that thing, Eyeball?"

"Oh, it's just a guy thing," Louis responded. He lowered the divining rod and walked over to his tent to unroll his sleeping bag.

Toni noticed the concerned expression on Ronny's face.

"What? What is it?"

"Well, you heard what Eyeball said about something strange out here?" Toni nodded that she remembered. Ronny continued, "It sounds as though he believes the cops don't know everything."

Toni shivered, and said, "I can't wait to wake up to the

morning sunlight." She brightened and grabbed his arm.

"Then we can visit the cave and see that everything's all right. That's what we need to do. Go to sleep."

After everyone settled into their tents for the night, the quiet and not-so-quiet chatter began. Thirty minutes after that, the talk was more hushed and more conspiratorial. Thirty minutes after that, Tom and Vince were competing with each other with snores. The girls were silent, and the boys in Rock's tent were quiet as well. Things were different in Ronny's tent. All three boys remained dressed and sitting Indian-style on top of their sleeping bags.

Louis and Jeremy managed to patch up their differences enough to talk about the idea of sneaking out of the tent, now that the adults had gone to sleep. Ronny wasn't against it at all. He encouraged it.

"Where do you guys want to go?" he asked.

Jeremy was excited now that some real adventure presented itself. His earlier fears seemed to have vanished although inside, he felt shaky.

"OK . . . OK." Jeremy stammered. "You guys probably want to go to the cave . . . right?" Ronny and Louis failed to respond immediately, so Jeremy took it as a yes. "Well," he continued, "if we're stupid enough to be here, this close to the cave where people were recently killed, then I guess more stupidity is expected. So, why not?"

Ronny shook his head.

"Come on, guys, why don't we wait until tomorrow?"

Louis had a surprising answer to Ronny's question. This was especially interesting since Louis was the one that thought the cave was haunted.

"If we go to the cave tonight we can look anywhere we want

without any adults around to tell us where *not* to go. We can do it quickly and then get back here pronto. Right?"

Jeremy answered, "We have to ask Rock to come along, just in case we need muscle." He considered a moment, frowned and then added, "we'll probably have to take Hawks and Larry just to keep their mouths shut."

Louis quickly interjected, "No girls. Agreed?"

As if on cue, the tent flap opened, and both Lorraine and Toni jumped into the tent and closed the flap after them. The boys were startled.

"What are you doing here?" Louis demanded. "We could have been naked or something."

The girls fought down their giggles.

Toni said, "Gloria and Pat are already asleep. We snuck out. I think Vince and Tom are asleep too."

Louis rolled his large eyes. "Great, now what?"

Lorraine knew something was up by the expressions on the boys' faces. "What are you guys up to?" she asked. "I see you still have your boots on."

Toni put the pieces together. "You guys are going to the cave," she announced. "Now, you *have* to take us with you. I'm not saying we'd squeal on you, but then again I'm not saying we won't, either."

Jeremy almost raised his voice and then quieted himself.

"No!" he insisted. "Too many people will make too much noise."

At that moment, Rock poked his head through the tent flap.

"Hey," he whispered. "You guys want to sneak over to the cave?"

Miraculously, all eight of them were able to sneak out of camp without waking any of the adults. It was easier and creepier than any of them had expected it to be. Once they were some distance away from the adults, Rock turned on his flashlight. One after another, the rest of them turned theirs on as well. The moon was high and almost bright enough to allow them to see where they were going without flashlights. Ronny whispered a caution for everyone to avoid shining any lights back at the tents.

Vivian watched from some distance away as the kids gathered in Ronny's tent, and then with renewed interest as they stealthily crept out of camp. A couple of hours earlier, Vivian had moved to a place near enough to the camp so that he could hear Tom's story. He loved scary stories. If he'd have titled that one himself, he'd have called it "The Cold Spot," named after the frigid shaft of moonlight Tom described at the story's end. During the story, he remembered the kid they called Brain, Jeremy, glancing at a little black box in his hand and pointing it straight in Vivian's direction. Vivian wondered if the kid could see him, but apparently, he could not. The kid looked concerned, scanned the desert with his eyes, and then went back to listening to the story.

Jeremy performed that same routine about an hour before that. This was at the same time that Vivian was drifting close to the camp. He was studying the colors emanating from their bodies. This was yet another so-called power that Vivian now possessed. Living human beings vibrate in frequencies that mirror and mimic their thoughts and emotions. He saw some promising traits in Theodore Hawks. Theodore had several inner qualities similar to Vivian's own. The colors he saw were close to crimson. Hawks appeared to be devilish, underhanded, conniving, rude, and selfish. At that point, Vivian decided to trade Martin in on a younger body. Preferably, this young Hawks kid if he could swing it. Who could tell how much longer Martin would be of any use?

Speaking of Martin, he thought, *I'll have to get back and move him around a bit, to keep him warm. Otherwise, that body might die before I'm ready to let go of him.*

Vivian was besieged by anxiety every time the black vortex appeared. He had no way of determining what it intended for him. The pulsing tornado-like funnel opened a black maw in his direction each time it reappeared and seemed determined to tug all the more insistently on him with each occurrence.

Vivian saw a distant "white light" vortex only once since he'd changed form. It appeared high in the air and whirled with what looked like brightly colored stars. Since then, this cursed black vortex kept reappearing. Because of the black vortex, Vivian was forced to remain in Martin as long as possible and caused him considerable paranoia whenever he was ethereal. The only way to escape it was to flee back into Martin.

Again, Vivian felt the imminent return of the vortex. The air around him started to pound and throb. He fled ahead of the kids and entered Martin at the spot where he'd left him last, at the location where he buried Beverly Winston. For some strange reason, he felt persistently drawn to that spot.

Martin/Vivian stood shakily up onto his feet. He pushed dirt and a lock of hair out of his eyes and then clamored down the slope. Vivian's plan was not yet fully formed in his mind. He decided to improvise. First, he needed to see what those brats intended to do at the cave, and then he would play with them. He experienced Martin's facial muscles tug into a smile as his mind conceived of a rough plan, with plenty of room for spontaneity.

It was an easy twenty-minute walk to the Wind Cave and quicker if they ran. Halfway there, Jeremy, Larry, Toni, and Lorraine started to have second thoughts about leaving camp.

Lorraine whispered, "I think we should go back now. I don't like it out here, and it's cold." She was shivering despite her jacket. Toni walked over and stood next to her. She enforced Lorraine's argument by adding, "They're going to wake up and find out we're gone. Let's go back."

There was no way that Louis would quit now that they were this close; however, he felt safer in numbers and said so.

"You guys can't go back. We need everyone. Besides, I think it's safer this way. Nothing's going to bug us if we stay together."

That was the wrong thing to say.

"What do you mean? We'll be safer?" Jeremy demanded.

"I mean just that," Louis explained. "Besides, if you go back, that's only three or four of you going back. Any wild animals out here would be more likely to bug you if there's less of a group. Wouldn't you rather wait a little longer and go back in force? Eight is better odds."

That logic was enough for now. They pressed on in silence, listening to the night sounds all around them.

There were bats, crickets, other chirping things, and an occasional coyote that howled at a comfortable distance away. A few minutes later, they were in sight of the single tree that Ronny remembered marked the entrance to the Wind Cave.

"There it is!" he announced.

Lorraine looked around, scanning the silent desert with her flashlight. For a fleeting moment, she thought she saw a human shape flitting between the shadows. She jumped a little and strained her eyes to find it again, but if something was moving, it was not moving anymore.

Ronny was excited. "It looks safe enough to me. What do you guys say we split up? Four of us will check out the main entrance while the other four go to where they found Beverly's body---over there."

Jeremy voiced a whispered hesitation that they all felt.

"What about sticking together? I thought you said that was safer."

Ronny shrugged. "I know, but I think it's safe, I mean, the coyotes seem far enough away. Besides, we can cover more ground this way and then compare notes. We'll meet right here in fifteen minutes. Hey, think about the stories we can tell all of the chickens that wouldn't come along on this trip."

That did it. Suddenly everyone felt brave enough to split up into two groups. The sheriff did say that all the murder suspects were locked up or dead. They could make this quick and then go back as heroes for doing this in the dead of night.

"All right, Normal," Hawks said. "What are we looking for?"

"That's the beauty of it," Ronny replied. "Nothing. Just look around, and then we'll go back to camp. No big deal, but we can say we did it, and we did it at night as I said."

They all agreed. Ronny led Jeremy, Toni, and Louis to the smaller cave opening, where Beverly was found; while Rock led Lorraine, Hawks, and Larry, to the main entrance.

Vivian/Martin was nearly seen by one of the girls. He was running between juniper trees when she turned her flashlight in his direction. Immediately, he dropped to the ground and waited until they resumed walking toward the cave. It looked as if they were heading toward the main entrance. *Perfect*, he thought. *I'll take Martin back to the other exit, and leave him there again. With any luck, the vortex might leave me alone for a while.*

He ran as quickly as he could, causing minimal noise. He kept reminding himself that a younger body might get him out of this cursed desert and into a city where there would be plenty of potential host bodies. He might have to injure Hawks a little to make his conscious mind docile, but then they would take him to a hospital which would present a new set of options.

Vivian arrived at the smaller cave opening and let Martin drop to the ground. For a moment, he considered the fact that he was doing Martin a favor. If it weren't for Vivian's possessions, Martin might have died from poor circulation. As it was, Vivian could feel Martin slowly regaining consciousness. It mattered very little to Vivian whether Martin woke up, or not as long as Martin didn't wake before Vivian got his new skin.

He checked to make sure that his hammer was still with him. It dutifully materialized in his hand and then winked out as he willed it gone. *Time to have some fun*, he thought and flowed through the opening into the cave.

Back at camp, headlights from another vehicle approached the campsite. Gloria Hawks and Patricia Powers were the first to wake as its tires crunched over rocky ground. Gloria rolled over and made the shocking discovery that the two girls were gone. She shrugged it off a second later thinking that they were probably out using the bushes for a nature call. Patricia leaned up on her elbows, unzipped her sleeping bag and the tent flap, and peered out at their visitor.

Gloria asked, "Who is it . . . is it the sheriff?"

Patricia answered with a question of her own. "Who would show up this late?"

By this time, Tom and Vince were already outside their tent. The dust settled around a green Chevy station wagon. The headlights winked out in favor of bright moonlight. Chuck Tenant and his father stepped out, followed by Chuck's two friends, Mike Thorp, and Mortimer Kraski.

Mr. Tenant smiled and extended his hand to Vince.

"Sorry, we're so late, Vince. We had some car trouble. You all go back to sleep. We'll set up our tents and crash and then see you for breakfast."

Vince returned Mr. Tenant's friendly manner and gave the hi-sign to the three boys behind him. He said, "I don't think it would hurt any if you guys want to say hello to the boys. They're probably waking up from all of the noise out here." He nodded toward the boys' tents. "Go ahead, guys."

Patricia and Gloria emerged with their flashlights turned on. Patricia looked around the camp and asked, "Tom, have you seen the girls?"

Vince paused in opening his tent flap.

"No, but they must be around here somewhere. Where else would they go?"

Gloria walked over to one of the vans, opened the side door, and peered inside. They weren't playing or sleeping in the van. She called out to the two girls and waited for an answer.

Only desert silence answered back. Now she was extremely concerned and looked frightened.

"They're not here!"

Chuck called out for everyone's attention. Their eager eyes and flashlights pivoted in his direction.

"Hey! They're gone, and there are tracks all over the place going that way!" He pointed out over the desert toward the Wind Cave.

Ronny and his three companions remained watchful as they quickened their pace. It would not take long to get to the little cave exit where Beverly's body was found. Only a few minutes at the most. Their bravery crossed their minds more than once as they walked fast under a desert moon.

Rock and his group arrived at the main entrance. Their

first concern was safely navigating the rocky terrain. They remembered Ronny telling them that this was where he stood the day he and his father entered the cave. Rock remembered with some discomfort that Ronny told his father that they should not go any further into the cave and that there was something wrong inside. Now, Ronny's friends stood outside that same cave listening to the night sounds all around them and imagining more than they heard. They scanned the cave with their flashlights looking for anything that would give them an excuse to leave. A steady breeze passing through the cave sounded hollow but not frightening. There seemed to be little reason not to go in, so they did. Rock took the lead, followed by Lorraine, Larry, and Hawks.

In Ronny's group, Louis stopped walking and said, "Hey, you guys, hold up a minute."

He pulled his divining rod out of his belt and used it to scan the desert. Jeremy nearly died of laughter. Toni jammed her elbow into Jeremy's ribs to shut him up.

"Ouch!" Jeremy managed. "What did you have to do that for?"

Toni frowned and held a finger up to her lips.

"Shhh!"

Jeremy glowered at her and rubbed his ribs. Louis scanned the area with his divining stick again and stopped studying almost immediately. The stick seemed to move in his hands. It pointed directly in the direction they were headed.

"There's a ghost up there," Louis whispered because he could barely breathe. "It's directly in front of us."

Jeremy almost hit him. "Throw that stupid stick away! I'm not even going to double check it against real science."

Louis huffed and rolled his eyes, then spoke in a sarcastic tone.

"You mean that pathetic little toy of yours? I thought you said that any schematic they would print in a magazine like the ones I buy would never work. Now you tell me that they *do* work. Is that what you're saying? What a jerk."

Ronny interrupted.

"Maybe your stick sees Beverly's ghost. It could be her out there." He glanced around and saw blank stares, so he added, "Well, it *could* be. Let's at least check it out," then turning to Toni; he asked, "Are you all right with this?"

She nodded and reminded him that being a girl didn't make her a wimp.

Rock's group agreed that their goal was to catch a glimpse of the hole hollowed out in the ceiling. Once they saw what Ronny had described, they would leave with their curiosity satisfied. Not long after entering the cave, Rock shined his light over what they now understood to be called the Dark Hole, which is what it looked like from the surface. He told everyone to turn off their lights.

"Shut 'em off a minute. I want to check something out." They all hesitated before turning them off. When darkness enfolded the group, Rock pointed out what he thought he saw.

"See? Look at the shaft of moonlight coming down through the hole. Doesn't that remind you of the story that Tom told us?"

He walked up to it and put his hand and waved it around.

"It even feels a little cold."

Lorraine felt her skin crawl. A shaky whisper was all she could manage in reply to what Rock had just said.

"That's just because there's wind blowing through there. You know that, Rock."

Rock nodded and smiled halfheartedly. They were about

to turn their lights back on when suddenly Larry shouted. He sounded frantic, and his voice cracked.

"H-hey, g-guys, there's something back there!" He pointed back into the pitch black depths of the cave. His finger was as shaky as his voice. "D-do you see it . . . something red?"

They turned on their flashlights. Now they were petrified. Their eyes darted around the cave, trying to see what he was freaked out about. No one but Larry saw anything out of the ordinary.

"What the . . . where?" Hawks demanded.

Larry was still pointing and backing himself toward the cave entrance, his face a mask of horror. All of their eyes turned to follow Larry's wide-eyed gaze. The cave felt ten degrees colder all of a sudden. Larry wasn't waiting for them to verify what he'd seen. He turned around and ran through the entrance.

Louis put his divining stick back into his belt as they approached the spot where Beverly's body had been found.

They all shone their lights around in paranoia, before letting them illuminate the small, dark, rear entrance to the Wind Cave. What they saw leaning against the hill next to the opening caused them all a scary moment of panic. Martin lay unconscious in an uncomfortable heap. He looked as though someone had tossed him aside like a broken doll.

Toni brought her hands to her mouth in a gasp. Louis froze. Jeremy took several steps backward, as though ready to run. Ronny thought Martin was dead and therefore safe enough to approach. He nudged one of Martin's booted feet with his toe while shining the flashlight into his face. Martin's eyes were closed, and his face and hair were caked and matted with dried blood. The foot moved without stiffness and Ronny thought he saw Martin's eyelids flutter.

"He's not dead," Ronny announced. "He's unconscious. I

don't get it."

"I do," Louis stated flatly. "I think I know what's going on here." He pulled his stick back out of his belt and pointed it at Martin. The stick turned in his hand and looked at the cave entrance next to Martin. "The ghost is in there now, but a minute ago this thing was pointing here at this place. I think that the ghost *possessed* this guy. It keeps moving him around. That's why no one found him. I think this is Martin. The ghost came out of him and went into the cave." Louis's voice grew shaky. He wagged his head and asked, "Why would it do that?"

Jeremy would not merely stand there and accept all of this from Louis.

"And how do you know that?" Jeremy demanded. Louis replied with unveiled contempt.

"You expect me to know this kind of stuff. Don't ya?" He looked down at Martin. "Well, I've read about something like this in those magazines you make fun of, Brain. You know the ones. Like the one you ripped the schematic for your box out of." Jeremy was uncharacteristically quiet, so Louis continued. "Somewhere out there may be a powerful force." He pointed the stick at the desert around them. "It might be dragging the ghost to someplace like heaven or hell, and the ghost doesn't want to go, so it steals a body to possess. From the looks of the dried blood all over him, I'd say Martin got clobbered senseless before the ghost took him over. Maybe that's what the ghost needed to take him over and run his body. Otherwise, Martin might interfere with his mind. You've heard stories about how possessed people try to hurt themselves. The ghost, in this body, has been running from the cops and heaven or hell, which is why the cops didn't find him here. Martin is like a zombie or something. Anyway, as I said, those magazines have a lot of cool stories about this kind of stuff."

"Who is the ghost?" Toni breathed.

No one answered her, although they all felt they had the answer to that horrible question gnawing at their stomachs. They remembered what the sheriff said about that man they thought killed Beverly. Vivian Robert McManus was the name. He was subsequently run down by a truck not far from the Wind Cave. Maybe he came back to haunt the place. The idea that Vivian's ghost came here and attacked Martin and then took him over made about as much sense as any other guess.

Jeremy decided that now was the time to check his black box. He was almost fearless about it, hoping he could refute Louis. His rant was dashed to pieces by its blinking red light. Even science seemed to agree that Louis might be right. Jeremy had been talking about his fears, although he tried to deny them, until now.

Toni, Louis, and Ronny's eyes watered with tears of fright when they saw what Jeremy's box was trying to tell them. They were so terrified they wanted to cry. Hot liquid fear crawled up their throats as they fought to decide what to do next. At that moment, Toni's flashlight shone on something that glittered just inside the mouth of the cave.

Toni spoke breathlessly.

"Look, what is that?" She walked closer and studied something dusted with dirt and partially hidden by rocks. She bent down and picked it up. It was a silver music box.

After Larry dashed out of the cave, curiosity ruled the three he left behind. They searched the cave and watched the dancing shadows cast by their flashlights, searching for answers. There was nothing to see.

Hawks was disgusted. "What a chicken," he muttered. Lorraine and Rock turned to follow Larry. They walked a couple of yards when they heard a horrible sound behind them.

When they turned their flashlights toward the noise, they saw Hawks doubled up in pain with his flashlight lying at his feet. He moaned in unspecified agony, bubbling spit between his lips.

Lorraine hurried over to see if she could help Hawks. When she bent down, his noises stopped abruptly. He looked into her eyes. She pulled her face back and away from his bloodshot gaze, but not before he backhanded her hard enough to lift her off her feet. She landed in rubble several feet away. Rock quickly reached her side and helped her to stand. He was furious.

"What's wrong with you, Hawks? I ought to deck you for that. I think I will!" He stepped over to the now standing Hawks and swung hard enough to knock nearly anyone unconscious. Hawks was already moving away from the fist aimed at his head what Hawks did next caused Rock not to pursue him.

Hawks was acting so strangely that Rock could only stare in disbelief while Hawks started throwing himself against the cave walls. Next, Hawks tried to ram his head into a pile of boulders but not before Rock grabbed him, threw him down and tried to hold him to the ground. Hawks growled and bit at Rock's hands, face, and arms. Finally, Rock had to let go. Hawks jumped to his feet and followed Larry out of the cave. Larry heard all the noise and yelled into the cave from just outside the entrance.

"Hey, guys! What are you waiting for? Get out of there! I'm telling you there's a ghost in there, and it ain't Beverly. It's big and looks mean. Can't you see it?"

Larry ran back into the cave still yelling for Rock and Lorraine and was almost knocked over by Hawks as Hawks ran past him.

"What the . . . Hawks. At least you've got some brains. Rock, Lorraine, get your butts out of there!"

Rock and Lorraine passed Larry in their flight from the cave. Larry shook his head and shouted after them.

"About time!"

Rock wasn't interested in running back to camp just yet. There had been an ill-defined expression on Hawks' face. It looked as though Hawks were trying to either kill himself or knock himself unconscious. Something in his gut told Rock that Hawks was headed for the hole outside the cave. He caught a fleeting glimpse of Hawks' face as he looked longingly up through the hole, just before Hawks bolted for the exit.

Rock yelled for Larry to go back inside and catch Hawks if he jumped down the hole.

"I think he's gonna jump through the hole . . . CATCH HIM!"

Larry yelled back, "What . . . why?"

Rock insisted, "I can't explain it! Just do it, Powers! I think the ghost is in Hawks!"

Larry reacted quickly. He knew he saw a ghost in there, so he thought Rock might be right. Rock sounded sure of himself. Larry ran back into the cave with Lorraine running after Rock. Larry was out of breath when he reached the hole inside the cave. He heard the sounds of an intense struggle above his head. He turned his flashlight up and illuminated Rock as he fought to keep Hawks from throwing himself down through the hole. Rock held his arms around Hawks in a fierce grip. His hands were locked together around Hawks' midsection. Rock held him nearly suspended above the hole. He grabbed Hawks just as Hawks was about to jump into the hole.

Vivian/Hawks looked down through the hole at the boy below. He remembered this boy from spying on them at the campsite. *Larry Powers*, he thought. *Guess I'll have to make do with him.* Vivian flowed out of Hawks' body and was just about to course straight into Larry when Vivian was forced to pull up at the last second. Something, or someone, had come between him and his intended victim.

Beverly.

Larry was amazed to see an apparition he'd seen only once before. The ghost of Beverly Winston hovered between himself and the evil thing that had left Hawks and was now racing toward him! Larry saw the unwholesome crimson glow of Vivian's ghost as it left Hawks and shot down the hole straight at him. His arms lifted in a defense reflex just as Beverly moved in front of him. He was convinced that he'd been saved from something awful.

Outside the cave, Hawks no longer struggled as Rock pulled Hawks safely to the ground. Inside, Larry drew back away from the hole with one hand held up in front of his face and the other holding the flashlight on a scene that nearly defied description. Larry was sure that Ronny would have been able to see what he was now witnessing illuminated not so much by flashlight as by moonlight shining down through the hole. A silvery middle-aged, ethereal, manifestation of Beverly was eye to ghostly eye with a crimson specter much more prominent than she was. The other ghost possessed a horrible aspect, with a full mouth, a small nose and two blankly vacant holes where its eyes should have been. It slashed at her with talon-like fingers, and she fought back as best she could by hitting at it with her transparent fists. The fight was a contest of wills, not physical impact.

Beverly had a limited effect on Vivian until she said, "It was you, not Thomas!"

Vivian pulled away from her and laughed. Larry watched as neither ghost seemed to be gaining an advantage over the other, and then he heard music coming from somewhere deep inside the cave---tinny music.

Beverly turned her attention to the sound. Larry could hear her say something like, "That's my music box." The other ghost was also taken back by the sound, but instead of merely turning toward it Vivian raced off in that direction leaving Larry alone with Beverly Winston's spirit.

Ronny watched the blinking red light with his three companions. Slowly their eyes met. The moment froze. Numb reality said that Louis was right and Jeremy's fears were well-founded. Then they all remembered what Jeremy had said while they were at camp. He'd said that the light on his box had blinked earlier that evening. Suddenly they wondered if whatever was in the cave had been spying on them all this time. Toni turned her attention and her flashlight back to the music box in her hand. She called everyone's attention to it.

"Hey, guys. Would you look at this," she whispered. "It has a ballerina on top."

Suddenly, Ronny made the connection.

"That's it!" he announced. "This ghost must be Beverly's killer. I'm just guessing, but he might have stolen this from her house after he killed her. She was once a ballerina. Sometimes she even appears to me as a ballerina. This might have been hers!" He frowned and added, "This box wasn't here when the police investigated the area." He pointed at the place where Toni found the box. "It couldn't have been here, because it wasn't well hidden. It had to have been brought here recently." He paused to think again. "I don't know how he could have carried it with him though---unless----" Jeremy punched him in the arm to get him to finish what he was saying. Ronny ignored Jeremy's fist and continued. "He, it, must be a poltergeist. That kind of ghost can move and carry things around with them somehow. Guys, this is bad, really bad."

Toni forgot the music box in her hand long enough to ask,

"Don't you think we should warn the others?"

Louis said, "Absolutely and right now, let's go!"

Ronny stopped them.

"No, wait a minute."

He patted his jacket, looking for something. Finally, he pulled two clear vials out of one of his inside coat pockets and then uncorked one of them.

Jeremy asked, "Hey, what are you doing with that blood-sucking stuff?"

"You'll see," Ronny replied and knelt next to Martin. He poured it out in drops all over Martin's exposed skin. His companions watched as he then uncorked the other vial and added drops of that fluid to complete the blood-like chemical reaction. Under the light of the three flashlights, Martin appeared to be bleeding through his pores as though he'd come down with a hemorrhagic illness.

Toni started by saying, "Gross," but then asked, "Why did you do that?"

Ronny answered, "That poltergeist might not find Martin quite so appealing if he thinks he's deathly ill."

Louis wasn't so sure about it.

"If the ghost won't climb back into Martin, then where will it go? Don't answer that. I don't want to know. Come on! We'd better warn the others."

They ran down the hill, although Toni lagged next to the cave entrance. Curiosity got the better of her. She opened the music box. The little melody from the box disturbed the pregnant silence of the night rather than sounding delicate and comforting. Jeremy heard the music, muttered something about girls in general, ran back to her, grabbed the box, and then threw it back into the cave.

"Hey, what did you do that for!" she shouted at him.

Jeremy grabbed her hand and pulled her along. He was angry.

"Now you've done it," he said. "What if the ghost heard it? Come on, Toni, let's go!"

Throwing the box didn't stop it from playing. They could still hear it as they ran for the main entrance. Its music reverberated throughout the cave.

Larry stood as still as a statue. Vivian's ghost had seemingly gone after the mysterious music, but Beverly's spirit remained. The presence of both spirits lowered the temperature in the cave until it felt like an ice cave. Now that Vivian was gone, the air was fresh but warmer.

Beverly turned to Larry. She said, "I would tell you not to be afraid of me, but I see it's too late for that."

Larry couldn't reply. He was too frightened to speak. She continued.

"Larry, everyone must leave here tonight. Forces are trying to pull Vivian into another world, and it's only a matter of time before they succeed. If he does manage to possess one of you, he might escape those forces for a time, but not without leaving that host with a great deal of mental and physical damage. Run! Run, now! Leave the cave!"

Then, she vanished.

Larry was alone in the dark. He had dropped his flashlight due to the shaking in his hands. He reached to pick it up and heard a commotion outside. He saw flashlights, a lot of them, illuminating the main entrance. Larry gave up trying to find his light and stumbled for the entry, then froze. A hair-raising scream like the wail of a banshee echoed throughout the cave and out across the desert.

Larry turned around to look back into the cave after Vivian's shriek. He was so terrified that he wasn't sure he could move anymore. He tried, but his legs buckled twice, and he fell both times. Looking back at the cave entrance, he could see Ronny, Rock, Toni, Louis the Eyeball, Jeremy the Brain, Lorraine, and Hawks outlined at the opening of the cave. The scream they'd all heard had not been formed from a human throat.

Ronny said, "It must not have liked what it found."

Then they heard another sound. Everyone at the cave recognized the sound of Volkswagen engines and crunching gravel. Two familiar vans pulled into the parking lot, followed by doors opening and the calling out of their names. Now the runaways were relieved at being caught for stealing away from camp.

The Cool-Crew arrived at the cave entrance ahead of the adults. Chuck, Mortimer, and Mike heard Vivian's scream, or howl, along with everyone else. The first question they had as they ran up to the cave entrance was, "What was that?"

After finding Martin's diseased body, Vivian didn't bother to check him out thoroughly. He thought that Martin most likely died from a dread hemorrhagic illness. Why? Martin was in decent shape not long ago. Vivian wailed in rage over the inconvenience, and now, adding insult to injury, that familiar pounding in the air had begun again. Somewhere, the black vortex was looking for him. Vivian had to find another body and quickly. He looked down at the music box. It was undamaged but silent now that it had wound down. His poltergeist mind was set with resolve. He rematerialized the hammer in his ghostly left hand. It was time to stop kidding around. He swept back into the cave.

Rock ran into the cave to help his friend, Larry. Chuck and his two friends followed close behind. Outside the cave,

Hawks was weak and sitting on a boulder cradling his bleeding and aching head in his hands.

Lorraine and Toni stood to one side as Louis, Ronny, and Jeremy walked hesitantly toward the cave entrance intending to help Rock. They could hear the adults calling their names. Lorraine and Toni shouted a reply and raced to meet them. Inside the cave, things quickly changed from bad to much worse.

Vivian arrived and was now plainly visible to Larry beneath the Dark Hole, bathed in the shaft of moonlight. When Larry saw Vivian's evil crimson visage, he pushed away Rock's hands that were trying to help him stand, and again, Larry tried to flee. Rock still couldn't see the poltergeist. Larry screamed, tripped, and fell for his efforts, only this time he hit his head and passed out. This was fortunate for Vivian since he'd been trying to knock Teddy unconscious and now this stupid kid had done that to himself.

Vivian laughed. It sounded loud, hollow, inhuman, and frightful. Hearing this sound, all of the kids cried out in fear. Mike and Mortimer backtracked out of the cave. Rock tried to pick Larry up to carry him out.

Vivian decided it was time to generate a little more terror, just for the fun of it. He used his poltergeist powers to whip the dust up from the ground in a swirling cloud around him. He held the whirling earth close to him, which made Vivian visible, as outlined by the flying dirt. He formed the dust and debris into a tight cyclone allowing his horrifying countenance to be seen by all. It was in this guise that he rematerialized his hammer. It appeared to float in the air at the end of a tornado-like tendril arm.

Louis watched in helpless horror alongside Ronny and Jeremy. Suddenly, a realization occurred to him.

"Ronny!" he yelled above the shouts and screams coming from inside the cave. "The totem! Use the totem Chas gave you!"

Ronny stared at him a second, blinking in brief bewilderment, before realizing what Louis was reminding him about. He had no time to think about it. He reached into his pants pocket and pulled out the totem. He could hear the adults, led by the girls, gathering around him. He stepped forward into the cave with the totem held high over his head.

It quickly became apparent that Vivian wanted Larry. Vivian roared forward and swung the hammer to strike at anyone who would get in his way. It was Wallace the Rock who stood in his way. As Vivian's hammer slashed through the air, Rock ducked, narrowly avoiding the blow.

At this point, Vivian heard two things louder than anything else around him. The first sound was the pulsating rush of the vortex. It was now plainly visible to Vivian just outside the cave. Vivian could see it as it pointed its black swirling abyss in his direction. The other sound was a loud guttural voice calling to him from somewhere near the vortex. The kids in the cave heard something of the vortex and the voice, but not clearly. To them, these sounds were more like a disturbance in the wind, howling through the Dark Hole.

Vivian reluctantly tore his attention away from Rock, Larry, and the vortex, long enough to spot the source of the voice. What he saw caused him to back away and halt mid-swing in yet another swipe at Rock's head.

Ronny advanced and noted with relief that the ghost seemed to be backing away from his upraised totem. In the next second, Chuck Tenant was moving in on the ghost as well. Chuck was throwing rocks at the ghost while yelling at it to leave all of them alone. Ronny could only think how brave, and dumb,

Chuck was acting. For all of his bravado, Chuck was surely going to get his fool head bashed in by the next hammer blow. Vivian saw things quite a bit differently than everyone else. He saw a purplish black spirit rising out of something Ronny held up in his hand. This spirit was calling out Vivian's name.

"McManus! Vivian Robert McManus! Hear me! I have a deal for you that you cannot refuse!"

Vivian looked around to see if anyone else heard any of this. Not even Ronny heard it. The dark spirit had the power to reveal its voice to Vivian alone.

"McManus!" the featureless creature relentlessly repeated. "Are you listening to me?"

"Yes, I'm listening. What are you?"

"I am a demon trapped in this damned stick for so long now that I've forgotten how long I've been imprisoned. There is no time to talk. I have a deal that you must accept, or what humans call Hell will take you."

"No!" Vivian snapped in defiance. "All I need is to take another body."

The demon laughed.

"Fool," it said. "These mere children tricked you out of the one that you had. How do you expect to gain another?"

"What do you mean? They tricked me?" Vivian demanded. The demon ignored him. Vivian fought off his irritation as Chuck continued to shout and throw stones at him. If it weren't for this unexpected demon creature, Vivian would have killed Chuck out of hand. Although they couldn't hear the demon, the frightened children did hear Vivian's responses to the demon, but this only added to the confusion and chaos of the moment.

The demon persisted.

"You must take my place in the totem, allowing me to enter

the portal in your stead. I've been to hell before, and I'll find a way to leave there again. You, however, would never be able to leave. You are not the same creature I am." The demon shouted for Vivian to make up his mind. "CHOOSE, McManus! You MUST choose *NOW*!"

Vivian became aware of an unrelenting power surging through the vortex, drawing him toward it. Judging by its insistent strength, he knew it would take him this time for sure. In that instant, Vivian made up his mind and hesitantly agreed.

"YES! DAMN, YOU! YES!"

The demon roared in triumph, then cried out, "DONE!" Vivian shrieked and felt himself being pulled forward through the cave, inexorably drawn to Ronny's totem. There was a cloud above Ronny's head; only Ronny could see. Vivian was being pulled to the totem, which attracted all of the strength Vivian had. The poltergeist that was Vivian McManus felt impotent. He watched the demon's purple/black shape disappear into the swirling black tube, and then the vortex wrapped in on the demon and disappeared. Seconds later, the pounding roar of the vortex was drowned out and then replaced by the cheers of the kids around him.

The shouts of victory had nothing at all to do with the events that Vivian had just gone through with the demon. None of the living had seen anything of Vivian's interaction with the demon. What they did see was Chuck's bravery followed by the poltergeist's hurried disappearance. Ronny's ability to view certain ghosts did not translate to demons. As far as he was concerned, he, Ronny, looked like an ineffectual idiot carrying a little black stick above his head. He was disgusted with himself, the totem, and Chas for having given it to him. He shoved the totem back into his pocket, grumbled something about feeling stupid, and then rejoined his friends. They weren't paying any attention to him at all. They were all cheering for Chuck!

Rock slapped Chuck on the shoulder.

"DID I see you beat that thing with rocks and bad language? You got rid of it, Chuck. You're a hero!" He laughed, followed by Chuck's nervous smile. Not one of them knew what just happened. They only saw the result.

Between Chuck and Rock, they managed to lift Larry's inert body out of the cave. Tom, Vince, and Mr. Tenant hurried to help them transfer Larry into one of the vans. It looked as though Larry would be OK. He was already moaning a little.

Tom said he would drive Larry to the St. Charles hospital emergency room, in Bend. Several kids climbed in next to Larry, although they were told that they would have to be dropped off at camp. The others piled into the other van. Back at camp, Mr. Tenant offered to tuck Larry comfortably into the back of his station wagon and then take him into Bend himself. He would take Chuck and his crew along as well. Tom agreed. Stunned silence held everyone's tongue until they arrived back at camp, then the reality of what had just occurred started to sink in. There was also the nagging question of where the ghost was right now. As far as any of them knew, it had run off somewhere but could return just as quickly. No one wanted to stay anywhere near the cave, and a motel seemed like the only sensible solution. Predictably, there weren't any arguments against this idea.

While they all worked at cleaning up the camp to leave, Ronny walked over to the smoldering fire pit they'd dug. He grabbed one of the sticks of kindling they brought and stirred the coals until they popped back into flame.

Toni watched him. She walked over to ask him what he was doing.

"Hey, what are you doing? We're supposed to throw dirt on

it, not stoke it up."

Ronny regarded her a moment, then pulled the totem out of his pocket. He bent down and shoved the totem into the hot coals. He heard Toni's sharp intake of breath. Before she could ask him why he'd done that, he said, "I know, Chas gave it to me, and it's probably valuable or something. I might hate myself in the morning, but right I'm now burning this stupid thing. It'll make me feel better. I looked like an idiot walking into the cave holding it over my head. What was I expecting?"

He started to stand. She playfully pushed him back down and giggled.

"You did look a little silly."

They watched as the totem caught fire. It burst into flame, and then they both walked over to help Mrs. Hawks fold up her tent.

Smoke from the fire curled up into the night. Bats flew around the swirling dark plume, avoiding the smoke, and then continued off into the desert. Something that wasn't a bat followed the bats. Ronny glanced over his shoulder and noticed a shadow rise out of the smoke and then fly off with the bats. *My eyes must be tired*; he thought and dismissed it as his imagination.

From the moment the totem caught fire, the curse on the totem was broken. Vivian was free. He rejoiced at his turn of fortune. As far as he was concerned, there was no way he was going to hang around, thereby inviting that vortex to return for him. The demon had said that it would satisfy the vortex's need to take Vivian by taking Vivian's place in hell. Vivian felt confident that the demon was telling the truth and that his destination would have been hell itself, so he felt smug that he'd traded with the demon. He paused in the air before the bustling camp below.

Should he grab one of them? *No*, he thought. *Why tempt fate by hanging around here any longer*? That was it then. The spirit-form of Vivian Robert McManus flew off into the night in search of new beginnings. He'd gone several miles when he abruptly flew into something dark and the size of a two-story house that suddenly appeared right in front of him. He could not stop his flight quickly enough to avoid running right into it. He barely felt the drumming in the air before the much larger vortex swallowed him the way a large fish sucks a smaller fish into its mouth without a moment's warning. This portal was not allowing him any time at all to get used to the idea of leaving the world of the living. Vivian's transitional phase in this realm was over. He screamed out "WHY?" so loud and audible that it startled creatures both on the ground and in the air. He thought he heard a reply in that cursed demon's voice, "I LIED!" The demon laughed as Vivian circled into the abyss and remembered his earlier muse, "If good things felt this magnificent, then how would bad things feel?"

Like the smaller vortex had done with the demon, this vortex wrapped itself around Vivian and then grew smaller and smaller until it vanished altogether.

Back at camp, Louis thought he heard a scream. He glanced around at the others. They hadn't heard anything, so Louis shrugged and threw several folding chairs into a van.

Unveiled

They spent Sunday sleeping off their exhaustion and agreed to meet in the park on Monday. What was left of KAUS would be there and Hawks said he would try to get the remaining members of KRSPY to come as well.

Monday afternoon's gray sky and drizzle over the secret park meant that closing ceremonies for the spy clubs would have to be short. Spy and Hawks called all of their group members out to the park to watch Rock machete down the blackberry bushes surrounding the now not-so-secret clearing. At first, Hawks' bunch didn't want to come. They reluctantly assembled out of curiosity if nothing else. Alfred the Corpse, Tommy Crotch, Linda Lips, Raymond Cooley, Greg the Sack, Todd Buttinsky, and Frank Farter all heard Hawks recount his daring adventures at the Wind Cave. It was hard for them to swallow, even if it was their leader relating the story, so now they wanted to hear from the others who went along on that trip.

Hawks invited someone else that surprised everyone. He brought Katie Riley, the Salem Heights' bookworm. Everyone wondered what she was doing standing there with Hawks. Lorraine excused herself from speculating over this with Lisa and snuck up behind Hawks. He and Katie jumped when they realized someone was standing behind him. Lorraine politely greeted Katie and then turned to Hawks to ask a direct question that felt to Hawks like she hit a line drive right into his gut.

"Hey, Ted, why is Katie here?"

She smiled at Katie, who wasn't smiling back. Katie adjusted her glasses, brushed back her red braids, and looked decidedly nervous. She was somewhat taller than Hawks. She looked down at him in anticipation of his answer. Hawks was not at all pleased by Lorraine's forward tone or her question, although he should have expected it from her. The truth he would never dare tell anyone was that Katie had invited herself to the park. Unless he played this inning just right, Slugger Lorraine might win or complicate a game he had been playing for almost three years.

Hawks decided to field her question with a direct question of his own.

"Why? Why do you want to know?"

Lorraine grinned and batted her eyes, undaunted.

"Oh, I'm just curious."

Hawks pitched, "She's here to watch Rock chop up the clearing and talk about last weekend, like everyone else."

Slugger wore a knowing expression on her face. It was time to knock that home run right out into the left field.

"OK, Theodore. Cut the crap. I've figured everything out."

"What do you mean?"

"I mean Katie here . . . She's the one that gave you the spy idea in the first place. Right?" Slugger pressed the issue without waiting for an answer. "Everyone knows you've liked her since fourth grade. We also know that she reads spy books all the time. She has a complete collection of trading cards from that TV spy show *Get Smart*. I'd bet the KR in KRSPY is her initials . . . Katie Riley, followed by S.P.Y."

She looked at Katie and saw her blush. Lorraine was right.

Hawks looked at Katie and then back at Slugger Lorraine. The game was over. He shrugged.

"All right, Slugger," he admitted. "You got a home run on that one, you win, but don't tell anyone. OK?"

Katie interrupted. Her voice was firm when she looked at Hawks and asked, "Why, Teddy? Why shouldn't she tell anyone? What's the big deal? The club's finished anyway. Besides, you never even told me what KRSPY stood for. I would have loved it. I love it now, even if you are a jerk."

Lorraine smirked. *Teddy*? Katie called him *Teddy*? Katie's bookish face broke into a warm smile. She surprised Hawks with a quick hug.

Hawks blushed, struggled with embarrassment, and then noticed that a few of the kids had seen Katie hug him. One of them was Rock, who paused in one of his Herculean chops at the blackberry vines to wipe his brow and turn his head long enough to witness a rare moment right before his eyes. Rock grinned and waved at Hawks. Hawks returned his wave in acknowledgment with a barely lifted hand. He waffled a little and then made excuses to Lorraine as to why he didn't want her to tell anyone else about his secret. He explained, "I didn't want the guys to know. Please don't tell anyone."

Katie wasn't pleased with his explanation. To her mind, it sounded like Teddy was sorry that he'd named the club after her. She glowered at Hawks. Hawks looked back at her a little sheepishly. He had a lot of explaining left to do, only this time to Katie. Lorraine smirked and figured that now was the right time to go and to let the lovebirds alone. She wandered over to where Linda Nellis—alias, Linda Lips—was sitting on a park bench watching Rock at work.

Linda was startled to see her. Lorraine held up a hand.

"Relax, Linda," she said. "I see Greg is ignoring you over there. He's getting plenty of information from Jeremy and Louis, but I guess you want to know how things went last weekend too."

Linda's uncertain expression brightened. She smiled and

admitted, "Yeah, I'd love to know what happened."

Lorraine called Lisa over to join them. It seemed that all of the members of KRSPY and KAUS showed up for this gathering. While Rock chopped down the last reminder of their segregation, many of these grade school enemies started dialogs that would spark new and renewed friendships. One by one, they walked over to express condolences to Spy, Phillip, about his grandfather's passing away.

Ronny and Toni wandered off by themselves. Larry spotted them and thought they were edging themselves out to leave the park. He ran to catch up with them.

"Hey, Normal, wait up!"

When Larry arrived, Toni looked up at Larry's head and said, "That's a lot of bandages, are you sure you're OK?"

"Of course," he replied. "Or they wouldn't have let me leave." He changed the subject. "Guess what? Beverly visited me in the emergency room."

Ronny wasn't surprised, but Toni was astonished and looked at it. She asked, "What did she say?"

"Well, she wanted me to thank everyone. Also, she left this on my bedside stand and told me to give it to you." Larry handed the ballerina music box to Ronny, and added, "It just materialized next to my orange juice. Everyone who saw it on the bedside stand freaked out completely because it wasn't there a moment before."

Ronny studied the box in awe. He felt sure that at one time this was one of Beverly's most cherished possessions. Perhaps that was why she was able to carry it. Except for a few scrapes, the box was intact. Toni was wide-eyed and asked if she could hold it. Ronny handed it to her.

Larry had more to tell them.

"I don't know if you've heard yet, but a huge framing hammer was found in the cave. It was covered in dried blood. The cops think it was a murder weapon, maybe *the* murder weapon, and they're working on verification and fingerprints."

Ronny asked, "How did you hear about that?"

Larry shrugged. "My dad is a cop with connections, remember?"

Ronny shrugged and then asked,

"What about Martin?"

Larry looked lost in thought for a moment and then replied,

"You told us about the blood sucking stuff you put on his skin. Dad said they went back for him. When they found him he was just waking up and complaining about the mess on his arms and face. He's in the hospital now."

Both boys shared a knowing nod, but Larry said what they were both thinking,

"We know who killed that Pappy guy, but the police haven't cleared Martin as a suspect."

Ronny looked at Toni. She was holding her silence as if she was afraid of the subject.

Larry felt a little out of place all of a sudden, and added, "Hey, look you guys, I'm going to take off. See you around, huh?" With that, Larry ran over to where Pokerface Tim was milling around with Jimmy the Spit Goblin, Spy, and Melvin Wad.

After Larry left, Toni felt encouraged to take Ronny's hand. She still had the music box in her other hand. He quickly warmed up the nerve and went so far as to lean over to kiss her. She let him, and then they hugged. They walked to the park rather than riding their bikes. After waving goodbye to a few of their friends, they walked hand in hand out of the park together and into their neighborhood.

Their first stop was Ronny's place to pick up his bike. After that, they would pick up her bike and head over to Chas' house. Ronny had promised to tell Chas everything, although he would try to evade any talk about the totem and how worthless it was against evil spirits.

They were opening the side gate at Ronny's house when his little sister, Jan, came slamming out of the front door. She nearly ran them over as she tried to catch up to them. She had been watching all afternoon at the window for him to return from the park.

"Ronny, Toni. Look!" She held up a package of photographs. She was jumping up and down with excitement.

Ronny asked, "Are these the pictures I took at the cave?" Jan nodded vigorously, nearly out of breath, and said, "Yeah, Mom just picked them up. Look at the one you took of Dad! Look, look!"

Toni looked at Ronny and then down at the photos as Ronny shuffled through them looking for that one picture. Finally, there it was. Jan craned her neck for another look at the photo she'd already seen. When Toni saw it, she gasped. Ronny's knees nearly buckled. David was smiling up at Ronny through the Dark Hole, just as Ronny remembered it. However, floating next to David, and looking up at Ronny, was the ghostly shape of a ballerina.

Factual Notes

Although this book is fiction, the horrific murder, the two spy clubs, the fated trip to the Wind Cave, and many other events in this book were not fabrications at all. I extrapolated several major and minor fictional elements from what is implied by available evidence, memories, eyewitness testimony, and shared youthful fantasy.

If you wish to research this case, you will find some of what you need to pursue it right here in this book. The name of the Bend newspaper that ran the first article on Beverly's case is accurate. For the convenience of those who are interested enough to page back to the name of the newspaper, the issue number was 163. I have also included all of the available information I was able to gather from official and unofficial sources. Separating the facts from fantasy should not be difficult at all.

With the passage of years, several baffling loose ends remain to perplex the authorities to this day. I encourage anyone with information that could lead to final closure to come forward. Officially, Beverly's murderer remains at large or perhaps spirited away.